Christine's Promise

Christine's Promise

Prequel to the Aspiring Hearts Series

KAY MOSER

© 2016 by Kay Moser

All rights reserved. No part of this publication may be reproduced, stored in a retrieval system, or transmitted in any form or by any means—electronic, mechanical, photo-copying, recording, or otherwise—without the prior written permission of the publisher. The only exception is brief quotations in printed reviews. For information, please address Hartline Literary Agency; 123 Queenston Drive; Pittsburgh, Pennsylvania 15235.

The characters and events in this book are fictional, and any resemblance to actual persons or events is coincidental or is a fictionalized account of an actual event.

*In honor of Christine Carpenter Pigg,
my beloved friend and valued mentor*

Chapter One

"There has to be a better way!" Mrs. Christine Boyd insisted as she crossed the railroad tracks that divided Riverford, Texas, into two vastly different worlds. When she did so, she left behind the dusty, unpaved roads of the slums and the hodgepodge shacks that were considered homes by the poor. "Delivering a few loaves of bread and some ham is simply not enough. And that poor child in the Jones family! His leg...." She straightened her spine and pursed her lips. "It's 1885, for heaven's sake. Things have to change."

Billows of red dust floated around her as she stopped and stamped her feet on the beginning of the sidewalk of the "quality" side of town. Straight ahead of her stretched an orderly, tree-lined, brick-paved street filled with neat cottages, their flower gardens proudly displaying the tired blooms of late September. To her left, however, she saw dark clouds of smoke and knew that one of the landowners nearby was burning his fields. She cringed at the thought of the choking smoke further adulterating the hot air that refused to give up its hold on East Texas. "Those poor sharecroppers," she murmured. "They will be standing all day in the glaring sun tending a blazing fire!"

Hollyhocks, their leaves yellowed and their flowers nearly spent, and sweet-scented honeysuckle greeted her over the white picket fences as she resolutely started down the first block. She was eager to reach an oak tree that offered her a brief respite from the broiling sun. When she reached the shade of the tree, she gratefully stopped and lowered her basket to the ground. She untied the netting which she had used to cup her wide-brimmed straw hat around her face and shook it thoroughly.

"Sakes alive!" A chocolate-brown face, surrounded by white hair and beard, popped up from the flowerbed next to the fence. "Miz Boyd, what you doin' down here so early in the morning?"

"Just running errands, Cal, but I am glad I ran into you."

"But ma'am, you ain't been 'cross them tracks, has you? That ain't no place for a lady like you. What Mr. Boyd gonna say when he hear 'bout it?"

Christine smiled as she shrugged her shoulders. "Time will tell, but that is not what I want to talk to you about."

"Miz Boyd, you look powerful hot. I better get you some cool well water."

"No, thank you, Cal. I haven't time. I want to talk to you about that boy they call Nobo. Who is he related to?"

"Ain't related to nobody far as I knows. Old Nessy take care of him. I 'spect she think he be her son, but she ain't never been right in the head since the War."

"He has a badly infected leg that needs attention."

"Yes'm. He done had that a long time. Ain't likely to heal, I figure."

"I am going to send Moses down with some ointment, and I want you to put it on his leg twice a day."

"You wants me to do it?"

"Yes, I do. As you said, Nessy is not reliable. Will you help the boy?"

"Yes'm, I be glad to." He leaned closer. "I already borrowed some of Miz Johnson's yams for the boy—"

Christine heard the screen door slam, and Cal suddenly fell on his knees and started pulling weeds.

"Cal! Who are you talking to? I'm not paying you to stand around and—" Mrs. Johnson limped down the steps, shaking a broom at Cal. "Oh gracious me!" She stopped in her tracks when she saw Christine Boyd. "Why, Mrs. Boyd, I had no idea...." The gray-haired, severe-looking woman dropped the broom, brushed off her apron and hurried forward.

"Good morning, Mrs. Johnson," Christine smiled as she retied the netting around her hat. "It is already a hot morning, isn't it?"

"Yes, and it doesn't help that Mr. Pritchard just has to burn his fields today."

"Yes, I was just thinking about the poor sharecroppers—"

"Oh, they're used to it, I figure." Mrs. Johnson waved her hand contemptuously. "If they aren't, they can just go back to where they came from."

"To Europe? That's quite a distance."

"No one asked them to come here in the first place. I'm not going to worry about the likes of them, but you, Mrs. Hodges, you shouldn't be out in this heat. I'll send Cal to fetch a bucket of cold water from the well for you. Cal!"

Cal jumped to his feet. "Yes'm?"

"What's wrong with you, boy? Blabbing your head off and keeping Mrs. Hodges standing around in this heat. Go fetch a bucket of cold water this minute!"

"You are most kind, Mrs. Johnson," Christine interrupted, "but please don't bother." Christine patted the large basket as she picked it up. "I've brought water for myself."

"I got the best well on this block. In fact, the biggest burden of my life is keeping the coloreds away from it. They don't think a thing about sneaking over here in the middle of the night and—"

"I'm sure your well is very tempting indeed and so much healthier than the river water available to them."

"No doubt, but I didn't dig that well for colored folks to pilfer the water—"

"I am so pleased you are sharing it with those who need it," Christine interrupted the woman.

Mrs. Johnson cocked her head and squinted at Christine.

"And I am sure I can count on you not to be angry with Cal. It was my fault he stopped working. I asked him to do me a favor."

"You asked Cal? Why, he's just a no-account colored. I'll be more than glad to do the favor for you, Mrs. Boyd. What is it you need done?"

"I need someone to apply ointment to a colored boy's leg twice a day."

Mrs. Johnson's head jerked back as her eyebrows shot up. "Well now, Mrs. Boyd, surely you know that no decent woman is going to touch a dirty—"

Christine held up her gloved hand. "That is why I have asked Cal to handle the situation for me."

Silence fell between the two women, and Cal stared at the ground.

"I am sure you will forgive me, Mrs. Johnson, if I cannot stay and visit longer." Christine smiled as she began to walk away. "I have one more stop to make, but I certainly look forward to seeing you in church tomorrow." She looked back over her shoulder and nodded her farewell to Mrs. Johnson.

"Well, of course," Mrs. Johnson called after her. "I don't ever miss church. Cal! Why in the name of heaven are you just standing there, boy? If you don't have enough work to do, I can sure find you some more."

Chapter Two

By the time the sun cleared the horizon, the Novak family had been picking cotton two hours. Jana Novak was still haunted by the memory of her sleepy little boys, their exhausted bodies swaying, staggering after their father as he walked down the rows of cotton in the pre-dawn darkness. In spite of the humid heat, she shuddered. What kind of world allowed—no, required—boys of seven and eight to be forced from their pallet on the dirt floor of a shanty and out into a field to work before the sun even rose? She felt a tugging at her skirt and looked down at four-year-old Josef. Tears were running down his cheeks, and he was holding up his arms to her, begging her to carry him, but she doubted her own strength.

"I can carry him," Sally offered. "He's not too heavy."

Jana studied her daughter's six-year-old face. Even the darkness could not hide its gauntness, the skin stretched tight across the cheek bones, the dark shadows under the large, protruding eyes. Love surged through Jana.

"Let him walk," her husband, Kazimir, called back without even slowing his gait. "You're already carrying the one inside you. I don't want you losing no more babies."

"What about these babies?" Her shrill voice sliced through the darkness. "For heaven's sake, Kazimir, they are children!"

He stopped but did not turn to face her. "Not any more, they ain't." His tone was flat, hardened. "They gotta work the fields just like I did back in the old country."

"Kazimir.…Look at them. They're hungry; they're exhausted. They can't go on like this. We need help."

"I don't see none coming, and if we don't get this cotton picked, we ain't even gonna have what we got. Mr. Lynch is gonna throw us off his land. Come on, boys! That sun's gonna be up 'fore we know it."

"Something has to change, Kazimir!" Jana shouted at her husband's back.

He whirled around and glared at her. "Well, I tell you what you do, Jana. You talk to that God of yours 'cause ain't nobody else listening." He pushed the boys ahead of him and turned back to the horizon. "Keep going, boys! We're gonna start right up here. I figure we'll make it to that old oak by noon."

Josef whimpered, and Sally picked him up and staggered down the row under his weight.

By nine o'clock the brutal September sun had dazed Jana. Perspiration dripped down her face, burning her eyes so thoroughly she could barely see Josef sitting in the dirt close by staring blankly into space. She gritted her teeth, squatted in the dirt and mechanically reached her numb, scarred hands forward. The plants had become a blur of white, and thus her fingers had become helpless victims to the thorns. Still she worked on, mechanically wrenching the fluffy white cotton from the stalk and stuffing it into the long sack that Sally dragged for her. It was only when Sally cried, "Mama, you're bleeding" that Jana knew she had been pierced enough to wipe her hands on her blood-dotted apron. The overseer would discount or reject cotton with blood on it. He would use any means to lower their end-of-season wages, any excuse to throw them off the land. And they had no other place to go. No one would hire them in the winter that was coming. If they lost this job, they would spend the cold months living out of their wagon in the woods.

She scrambled further down the row and kept picking.

Jana had previously given birth in inhospitable places—in the back of a wagon, in the row of a cotton field, and under a tree—but those births had always come in the warm months. Her next baby would be born in the dead of winter.

In spite of the blistering heat, she shivered violently. Sally dropped the sack and threw her arms around her mother's neck.

"Rest, Mama!"

Jana clung to the six-year-old girl and looked around her. Her world had become a white haze, a blur of the acres of white cotton flowing into the white heat of the sun. She could barely discern small dark spots close by, which she knew to be her husband and her little boys laboring, suffering.

"God in heaven, have mercy on them," she whispered as she dragged herself forward, squatted and reached toward another fluffy white ball. "They are children! They need rest, water, food."

The thought of food for her children sent her mind spiraling into panic. She had lugged buckets of water from the stream to the dying vegetable garden last night after everyone else had collapsed on the dirt floor of the shanty and sunk into sleep. By the light of the moon, she had dug up the last of the yams and picked the drying black-eyed peas.

She tried to thrust her hands toward the plants, but they would not obey. They began to shake. Confusion conquered her, and she registered nothing more until she felt the jolt of her head hitting the ground.

"Get her into the shade, Sally!" Kazimir's commanding voice broke through her mind's numbness.

She felt someone tugging on her hands and understood that Sally was trying to pull her up. She sat, pulled her legs under her, and felt Sally's small body under her armpit struggling to push her up. Her vision cleared slightly, and she saw little Josef lying facedown in the dirt. Panic roared through her, and she stood.

"Josef!"

"He's asleep." Sally panted beside her. "Come on, Mama. We gotta get you to the tree. I'll come back and get Josef."

"No...no. I can walk." She willed her legs to move. "Don't leave Josef."

"I'll bring him."

"And the water."

"It's under the tree. Don't you remember?"

Jana buried her head in her hands. *God help me. I don't remember.*

"Walk, Mama." Sally pushed her toward the shade of the oak.

Jana turned around and saw Sally pull her little brother to his feet, squat down, and pull him onto her back. Her heart broke, and tears she did not know she had left streamed down her face. *Help me, God! I don't know how to save them.*

"Walk, Mama." Bent over by the weight of her brother, Sally staggered ahead of her mother. "Please, Mama. Just walk."

When Jana reached the tree, she sank to the ground and drank from the earthen jug of water. Her head swam, and her whole body begged to lie down, but she dared not recline for fear she would not be able to get up again. Instead, she propped her elbows on her bent knees and held her dizzy head in her hands.

Sally gave Josef a drink, then he crawled to Jana's side, lay his head in her lap, and slept. Sally knelt at her mother's side and solemnly gazed into her face as Jana waited for her head to clear.

When Jana could think again, she squinted her eyes against the glare of the field and watched her boys struggle to keep up with their father's pace. Kazimir was picking cotton as if his life depended on it. And it did. His life and the lives of his family. *He's a good man. He loves us. He's pouring out his life for us as surely as if his blood was running into that red soil. But it's not enough. It will never be enough!*

She looked at Sally's dirt-smeared face with its eyes that were far too old for a six-year-old child. She was startled by the fierceness she found there.

"We need help, Mama."

Jana looked down at the weakened, undernourished child in her lap and back at her sons, her children, working in the blistering sun. *She's right. Lord, something has to change. We cannot go on like this. Help us!* Seconds later she knew that whatever help God had in mind, He expected her to walk toward it. To walk away from the failure of the present, the hopelessness of depending only on themselves.

She set Josef aside on the dry grass, and struggling hard, she stood.

"Kazimir!" she shouted. "You and the boys come into the shade and have some water."

"We gotta work our way to that shade, Jana. Ain't no other way to get this cotton picked."

She knew it was hopeless to argue with him and redirected her attention to her sons.

"Boys, come drink some water." The boys looked at their pa, who motioned them toward the tree. They dragged themselves toward Jana, and when they reached her, eagerly accepted the jug she held out.

"Now listen carefully, boys." Her voice was firm. "I'm gonna go into town."

The boys silently stared up at her, disbelief painted on their faces.

"I'm taking Sally with me and leaving Josef here to sleep under the tree. I want you boys to keep an eye on Josef and be sure y'all keep drinking water. When the sun is overhead, I want you to come eat this corn mush and beans and rest for a while. Do you understand?"

"Pa ain't gonna let you go to town," Norbert, her oldest, insisted.

"I don't plan to ask him. I'm gonna find some work."

Norbert turned on his heel and ran out into the field to his father.

Jana steeled herself as she watched Kazimir throw down his cotton sack and storm up the row toward her.

"Have you lost your mind, woman?" he yelled as he advanced on her.

"No."

"*Jsi šílený!* You've lost your mind. Ain't nobody gonna hire you. What're they gonna hire you to do?"

"Wash clothes, help them with canning, clean house—whatever they need done."

"And you think them town folk are gonna give you cash money to do that?"

"They'll at least give me food."

"My wife ain't gonna go to town begging."

Jana lifted her chin and met his eyes. "You're right. She's gonna go to town to work."

"*Vaše myšlení je hloupý!*"

"Don't call me stupid!"

"Jana, you ain't thinking straight. Those town folk don't care nothing about us. They just as soon we die out here. Have you forgotten that Mr. Lynch ain't paid us in months?"

"Of course I ain't forgotten."

"Then what makes you think them town folk are gonna give you anything?"

"I ain't gonna talk to the likes of Mr. Lynch. I'm gonna talk to the women folk."

"Jsou právě chystá smát!"

"I've been laughed at before. I survived then; I figure I'll survive again if I have to. Things have to change. Maybe you're wrong. Maybe I can find work. I won't know till I try." She took Sally by the hand. "We're leaving now."

He stormed away but called back, "Well, you ain't no good in the field, that's for sure."

Chapter Three

Christine sighed as she hurried through the thickening smoke toward the center of town. "Why is it that the more needy people are, the more untouchable they become? Is it really so hard to see beyond the dirt? To see the suffering human?" She thought of Cal's immediate willingness to help Nobo. "Those who have the least seem to be the most compassionate."

The houses became more substantial, two-storied, porch-draped refuges of comfort set in large gardens. The simple, white picket fences gave way to ornate, iron enclosures, and the flowers that greeted her were pampered roses, regal hydrangea blossoms that had turned rose and green in the heat, and beds of verbena.

A hot breeze sent dry, curled oak leaves clattering down the sidewalk in front of her and brought a waft of choking smoke. She coughed and tried to fan away the heated, smoky air before it could send her mind reeling back in time to a war-ravaged place she hated to visit. It was too late. The past overtook her; the images of her childhood suffering in Charleston during the War ballooned in her mind; the present morning in sleepy Riverford, Texas, faded.

She was a child of nine again, and the streets she stumbled through—dragged along by her frantic mother—were darkened by smoke, a thick charcoal layer occasionally lightened by roaring flames darting out from a building. Deafening, explosive sounds assaulted her ears so painfully she desperately wanted to snatch her hand away from her mother's and cover them. Instead, at her mother's shouted command of "Run!" she lengthened her stride, her slipper-encased feet pounding down on the cobblestone until they grew numb. She could not breathe. The smoke choked her, as her heart beat wildly and her sides ached, but still her mother dragged her on. She heard horses' hoofs, seemingly hundreds of them, clattering behind her, gaining on the two of them. Men shouted, their tones strangely eager and excited, while women screamed in terror.

Her mother banged on door after door, begging for shelter, but no door opened. The horses grew closer, and the men's shouted words became distinct. "Get them! Find the Gibbes woman. Find the girl. That rebel general will surrender when we have his family."

Christine suddenly understood why the men were chasing them. She started sobbing with terror, but her mother quickened her pace and continued to jerk Christine forward.

And then her mother's hand was suddenly gone. Christine was still propelling herself into the darkness, but the guidance of her mother's grip had been broken. She heard her mother cry out in terror. Then, silence.

A strong hand grabbed her as another hand slammed across her mouth. Her lips were lacerated by her own teeth as she was dragged into an alley and pulled to the ground. Her mother was there, unconscious, her head bleeding, and someone was kneeling over her, stripping off her dress. Christine struggled against the overpowering hands and tried desperately to scream.

Horses and riders pounded by out on the street, a deafening roar of hoofs striking stone, cursing male voices and occasional pistol fire. The alley shook under Christine and her captor. She fought for air, clawing at the man's face with strength she did not know she possessed. Abruptly he freed her, and she lunged toward her mother's unmoving body. The person ripping off her mother's clothing turned toward her, and through the smoke Christine saw a tear-stained female face. To her amazement, the woman opened her arms wide, struggled forward on her knees, and enveloped Christine in a loving embrace.

"We gonna save her," the woman promised. "Don't you worry. We gonna save your mama. You gonna help. Right?"

Christine nodded vigorously, and her pounding heart began to slow as she drew back and watched the woman raise her fingers to her lips and whisper, "Shhhh! No talking now. We gotta make you and your mama look poor like us. Soldiers ain't interested in poor folk. Right?"

"Mama's bleeding! Her head—"

"I know, honey. Ain't nothing but a scrape. Quick now! Take off that fancy dress of yours. I'm gonna get some old clothes for you and your mama." The woman struggled to her feet and limped toward an old wagon with a decrepit mule harnessed to it. Moments later Christine and her mother had been transformed into sharecroppers—their delicate, sprigged muslin dresses changed to homespun, their hair mussed, dirt applied to their hands and faces.

"You're just a sharecropper's granddaughter now," the woman explained as the man picked up Christine's mother and put her in the back of the wagon. "Your mama's my daughter, and she's very sick. You're my granddaughter. You understand?"

Christine nodded as the woman helped her climb into the wagon.

"But who are you?" Christine asked.

"I'm your Grandma, Anna Clayton, and he's your Grandpa, Ira Clayton. Can you remember that?"

"Yes, ma'am."

"Can't have none of that blood showing on her head," the old man said as he climbed onto the wagon seat.

"I know, I know." The old woman took Christine's fancy, ruffled dress and wiped the blood off her mother's forehead and face.

"Get on up here on the seat, woman," the man insisted "We gotta get going!"

The old woman threw Christine's dress on the ground next to her mother's and climbed onto the wagon seat.

The wagon began to rock behind the slow gait of the mule, and Christine stared at her dress, crumpled in the dirt of the alley, as the familiar neighborhood of her childhood began to fade into the smoke-filled darkness.

"Good morning, Mrs. Boyd!" A man called out from a passing carriage, and Christine was catapulted back into the present and Riverford, Texas.

When she attempted to respond, she discovered she was too breathless to talk. Her journey into her nightmarish past had exhausted her. She stopped and held on to a fence.

"They saved us," Christine whispered as she pulled a handkerchief from her sleeve and dabbed at the mingled perspiration and tears on her face. "For absolutely no reason other than love of fellow human beings, they saved us. We were strangers, but they saved us."

With trembling hands Christine opened her basket, withdrew the jar of water, and drank the last of it. Her thirst quenched, she surveyed the block and realized that she was only two houses away from the home of Mrs. Fanny Sharp. Quickly she drew in her breath. *Composure! I must regain my composure. One more block, and I will be at St. Paul's. There I can sit in the quiet and recoup myself.*

She put away the jar, straightened her spine, and created a content smile on her face. *Courage, Christine!* She surveyed the tall holly hedges that fronted most of the garden of the Sharp residence. Only the open area around the wrought iron gate presented a problem. *Perhaps I can just slip by.* She quickened her pace as she approached the gate.

"Why, it's Mrs. Boyd!" Fanny Sharp's voice jolted Christine's nerves as the woman bolted down the front steps of the porch. "Look, Clementine. As sure as I'm living, Mrs. Boyd is out walking in this heat."

"Mercy, no!" Clementine Drift raced past Fanny. "Mrs. Boyd, you *must* come up on the porch and rest yourself. Why, it's simply broiling!"

"Thank you, no. I must be on my way," Christine waved gaily as she kept walking.

"You *must* stop, Mrs. Boyd," Mrs. Sharp insisted as both ladies reached the gate. "What on earth are you doing out in this heat?"

"I had a few errands to run."

"Why aren't you driving your buggy?" Mrs. Sharp demanded. "Why, in heat like this, I wouldn't think of walking."

"Oh, I needed some exercise," Christine lightly responded. *My buggy would have made me far too conspicuous.*

"Exercise in this heat?" Mrs. Drift asked.

Christine laughed. "Well, it seemed like a good idea earlier although I must admit that now I wonder. Excuse me, ladies. I must be getting on."

Fanny Sharp transformed her face into a portrait of sad sympathy, opened the gate, and took Christine's arm. "We were just talking about your family, Mrs. Boyd. We've both been so worried. Have you heard from your dear father, General Gibbes? Has he found Charleston changed?"

Mrs. Drift shook her head slowly. "It must be such a bitter experience to return to a place he loved so and find it ruined. Especially after he led our troops so gallantly."

"And suffered those years in prison," Fanny added. "What a demeaning experience for him! Why, it's a miracle he was ever able to hold up his head afterward."

Christine's temper flared, and the heat of the sun diminished in comparison to the heat that surged through her.

"The dear, dear man." Clementine Drift's hand fluttered to her breast as her lips turned down and she shook her head in exaggerated sympathy. "Exactly how long was he in that horrid Yankee prison?"

"Far too long!" Christine snapped before forcing herself to regain her composure and smiling pleasantly. "I am sure Father is finding Charleston changed. It has, after all, been twenty years since the War ended."

"You mean you haven't heard from him?" Mrs. Sharp raised her eyebrows as she gave Clementine a meaningful look.

"Not even a letter?" Clementine pried. "How strange...."

"Oh, I don't think so, ladies." Christine made a show of shifting the basket to her other arm. "He has only been gone five days, but how very kind of you to be concerned. Now, I am certain you will excuse me. I have one more errand to run."

"Where?" Mrs. Sharp demanded.

"Fanny!" Mrs. Drift protested. "Perhaps her errand is personal."

"Not at all," Christine replied. "I am on my way to St. Paul's to play the new piano. The rector has asked me to evaluate it and determine if it needs adjustments after its shipping."

Mrs. Sharp drew her head back and snorted. "Hmmp! Why on earth would he ask you?"

Christine dug deeply into her self-control and managed to smile. "I have had a little experience with the piano."

"I should say so!" Clementine Drift exclaimed. "She practices hours and hours every day. Everyone knows that."

Mrs. Sharp narrowed her eyes. "How do you find the time for all that practicing, Mrs. Boyd? Your poor little boys must miss their mother so."

Christine laughed at the obvious jab. "My poor little boys are studying, then dashing out to play baseball. They are far too old to want to cling to their mother. Good day, ladies." Christine walked on and was quickly hidden by the holly hedge.

"She's not fooling me one bit," Christine heard Mrs. Sharp say. "She's been down across the tracks handing out food and heaven knows what else."

"Do you really think so?" Clementine Drift, sounding eager for gossip, encouraged Mrs. Sharp. "Do you think her husband knows?"

"I doubt it, and if you ask me, that's why she's walking instead of using the Boyd carriage."

"Oh, Fanny, how delicious!" The volume of Mrs. Drift's voice increased with excitement. "Think of the romance of it. Grand lady, daughter of General Gibbes and wife of respected town banker, sneaking around in the slums of colored town."

"I declare, Clementine!" Mrs. Sharp's voice rose angrily. "Sometimes I think you're addle-brained. There's nothing romantic about a lady creating upheaval in the social order. Why, the next thing you know she'll be helping those immigrant sharecroppers."

"She wouldn't!"

"She would! And if she does, she'll just be encouraging them to rise above their station. Why, I wouldn't put it past her to invite them to church."

"The immigrants or the coloreds?"

"The immigrants, you ninny! Not even Christine Boyd could get away with inviting colored folk to church."

Christine finally reached the corner, and their waspish voices became the mere buzzing of insects, but they had definitely stung her. She felt their poison raising welts of anger on her mind. *Who do they think they are, judging me? Are they completely empty of compassion for their fellow humans?*

Mercifully, a wagon rattled by, and the jarring sound diverted her mind. Once the wagon had passed, St. Paul's loomed just across the street, and her clear view of it activated her conscience. *Really, Christine! How can you think of descending to their level?* She crossed the street briskly and entered the courtyard of the church.

Chapter Four

Jana followed the dusty, sun-baked wagon road away from the fields and toward town. The sun rose higher, piercing her sunbonnet with its merciless rays; perspiration ran down her face, neck, and back, but she kept moving. One foot in front of the other…one foot in front of the other. She focused on the tiny bursts of red dust that each step scattered into the wind and counted each a victory as it brought her closer to help for her family.

Every time she looked down to check on Sally, she saw only the top of the little girl's sunbonnet and her short legs reaching for two paces to match each one of her own. *Dear God, help her. She's so small. Oh Lord, have mercy. She's just a little girl.*

Jana thought of turning back, of giving up her hope of finding work in town, but the memory of the boys still working in the field, still valiantly trying to match their father's determination, enforced her own. She gritted her teeth, wiped dripping perspiration from her face, and kept going.

They had almost reached the shade of a patch of woods when Sally stopped and started heaving. Panic shot through Jana, and oblivious to her own weakness, she scooped the girl up and carried her the last one hundred yards to the shade. *Water! Dear God, please give me water to cool her off.*

She stood still and listened. Yes, somewhere nearby there was water splashing over rocks or downed tree limbs. Jana searched the trees, looking for birds. They were plentiful, and many were swooping down toward the same spot. The water would be there. She calculated the destination of the birds' converging flights, and still carrying her daughter, she fought her way through the underbrush toward it. The sound of water grew stronger; her hopes increased.

When she reached the edge of the cheerful creek, she lay her daughter down beside it and removed the child's bonnet and tattered boots.

"Mama," Sally opened her eyes.

"Everything is gonna be all right, honey. You just had too much heat. I'm gonna put you in this creek. Don't be afraid. It's not deep, but it will help you cool off."

"You're hot too, Mama. You come in the water too."

Jana pinched her lips together to keep from crying and used the last of her strength to lay Sally in the creek. The child's long hair loosened from its knot and streamed out around her head.

Sally smiled up at her mother. "Come in, Mama. It feels good."

The smile on Sally's face was the medicine Jana needed. Her pounding heart began to slow. With shaking hands she untied her bonnet and the lacings of her boots and dangled her feet in the water.

"Come in and lay down, Mama," Sally encouraged. "It's cool."

"I can't get my dress wet, honey."

"Why not? It'll dry real fast when we go back in the sun."

Jana looked down at her dirty dress and had no problem imagining how oily her hair must be. "No one's gonna hire me looking like this," she murmured and began to unbutton her dress.

Sally giggled.

Jana stopped undressing, and tears filled her eyes.

"Mama, you're crying."

"Tears of joy, baby." She pulled her dress over her head. "How long has it been since I heard you laugh?"

Sally giggled again as she splashed in the water.

Jana joined her daughter in the creek, lay down, and pulled the hairpins from her bun. What bliss! The cool water flowed over her, cleaning and soothing her sun-scorched skin, drifting through her long hair. "I just wish the boys could be here."

"I don't think boys like to be clean as much as girls do," Sally observed.

Jana laughed. "You are wise beyond your years, little girl."

Sally sighed. "Just listen to the birds sing, Mama. I wish we could live in the woods forever."

"So do I, baby, but we can't stay long. We gotta get to town and find work." Memory of her purpose prompted her to sit up, reach for her dress, and douse it in the water. "It won't be a bit newer," she observed as she scrubbed the fabric, "but it'll be cleaner. That will surely count for something with town folk."

Sally gasped excitedly, then whispered as she pointed. "Look, Mama."

A group of butterflies were drinking from a bowl formed in a rock by time and the friction of moving water. A shaft of sunlight lit the bowl and spotlighted the large, yellow butterflies rimming it.

"Oh, Mama," Sally sat up and scooted toward her. "Do you think they live here?"

"They might. Or they might be migrating through this area."

"What's 'migrating'?"

"Traveling through as you move from home to home."

"No!" Sally's voice was forceful. "This is gonna be their home. They don't have to fly any further."

Jana studied the determination engraved on her daughter's face. "Why do you say that, honey?"

"Because they have everything they need right here. They have water and flowers and lots of places to make their cocoons." Sally vehemently nodded her head. "They're gonna stay here! There's no better place anywhere else. They just have to *decide* to stay."

Jana studied her daughter's determined face, and the wisdom of what the child had said slowly seeped into her brain. She and Kazimir had wandered like gypsies, settling in whatever sharecropper's shanty was offered to them. The result had always been the same; they were thrown off the land at the end of the season, forced to move and start again. Over and over and over.

Jana stood up and forcefully wrung her dripping dress. *This time we stay!*

"We better get going, honey. The sooner we get to town, the sooner I can find work."

Sally nodded her agreement, staggered to the edge of the creek and began to wring out the skirt of her own dress. Jana dressed, pulled on her battered boots and quickly laced them up. When she reached over to lace up Sally's boots, the girl put out her hand and stopped her.

"I want the butterflies to stay here, Mama, and I want all of us to stay with them."

"I know, baby. Let's go see if we can make that happen."

Chapter Five

When Christine entered the courtyard of St. Paul's Episcopal Church, the first thing she saw was a statue of St. Francis holding a bowl of water for the birds. Her anger with Fanny Sharp and Clementine Drift evolved into an attack of conscience.

"Oh dear," she muttered as she sank on a bench across from the statue and contemplated it. "How dare I even consider entering a church with such anger in my soul?"

Where there is anger, let me sow peace. The words of the famous St. Francis prayer filtered through her mind and aroused her conscience further. *I am absolutely hopeless! I have let two petty women infuriate me, and if truth be told, I am furious because of their personal attack, not because of their lack of concern for the poor.*

The heavy, carved door of the church creaked open and startled her out of her self-condemnation.

"Why, good morning, Mrs. Boyd," the rector greeted her. "Have you come to test the piano?"

"Yes. Yes, I have." She stood and did her best to look composed.

"Well, just let me fill this bird bath, and I'll be on my way and leave you in peace with the piano." He grinned at her as he hoisted a silver pitcher and began pouring water. "Don't tell the church ladies I used the baptismal pitcher. They'll be scandalized."

Christine smiled and was relieved to feel her anger with herself ebbing away. "Your secret is safe with me."

"Well now, come on in." He held the door for her, and she entered the cool, shadowy foyer.

"How wonderful," she exclaimed. "It is easily ten degrees cooler in here."

The rector tucked the pitcher at the base of the large, stone baptismal font before pointing to the stained glass window to the left. "I often think that window should read 'Come Unto Me All Ye Who Are *Heat* Laden.'"

Christine nodded. "More appropriate for many of us during a Texas summer, I am sure." She walked to the jewel-toned window and looked up into the compassionate face of Jesus. "I think, however, that for some of our neighbors the heat would be easier to endure if they were not so hungry."

He cleared his throat and changed the subject.

"In my opinion this is the finest stained glass window in Texas. As you probably know, the Hodges family built this church in 1838, just a few years after they came to town. The matriarch of the family was French—from Paris, in fact. Obviously a lady of exquisite taste. It was she who commissioned and paid for the windows in the church."

Christine turned and silently stared at him as tears gathered in her eyes.

"Have I said something to upset you?" The rector moved to her side.

"No." Christine wiped her eyes with the back of her gloved hand. "It just suddenly occurred to me—what I mean is...she was an immigrant."

"Yes, she was. She came to New Orleans as a young woman, and it was there that she met and married the grandfather of the current head of the Hodges family, Hayden Hodges."

"But she was an immigrant, and just look at the beauty she brought to this small town."

He nodded. "We were fortunate indeed that she came to Riverford."

"Yet we can find no reason to welcome the Czech and German immigrants in our midst."

He cleared his throat again. "It is a sticky issue. I'll grant you that."

"Should it be?"

"No." He shook his head sadly. "Our hearts should not be so closed."

"Nor should our financial assets."

"Well... uh... I must go." He fidgeted with the cuffs of his shirt. "I have several calls to make. I look forward to hearing your evaluation of the new piano."

He bowed slightly, turned, and left Christine alone with the window.

Heavy laden. She pondered the two words and considered how those words could describe so many human conditions. The dramatic needs of the poor. The indignity that the Coloreds carried on their backs. The anger, the hatred, the lack of forgiveness still lingering from the War. The nightmares and fears of those who had endured the war years. The illnesses, the griefs. The list was endless, and no one was exempt. They all needed their burdens lifted.

"And I must add the burden of my own anger with Fanny Sharp and Clementine Drift," she murmured. "I must choose to let that go."

She entered the sanctuary doors, walked down the center aisle, and made a slight bow of respect to the golden cross hanging behind the altar. Her mind was cluttered with the conflicting images of the morning, those which had occurred in Riverford and those she had remembered from her childhood. Her heart longed for its usual peace. *Lord, lift me up and let me stand....* The lyrics of her favorite hymn began to drift through her mind. She did not go straight to the piano; instead, she chose to settle her weary body on the front pew and wait for the divine refreshment she knew would come.

Gratitude began to flow through her mind and settle in her soul. *Thank you for that couple who rescued Mother and me so long ago. Thank you that Richard Boyd came into our lives and shepherded us through the years of trial, the waiting for Father's release from prison, and the move to Texas.* Christine's heart fluttered when she thought of that handsome young soldier whom she had loved at first sight when she was only nine years old. Amazingly, he had learned to love her, had asked her to be his wife, had fathered her two sons.

"How blessed I am," she whispered. "You, oh Lord, have delivered me from terrible trials. It is no less than a miracle that I sit here now in this beautiful church, the wife of a respected man, the mother of two sons. So many did not escape Charleston, or if they did, they escaped with grave injuries or they lost everything and sank into despondency. But I was rescued... against all odds."

Unconsciously she tapped her fingers on the wooden pew, imitating her memory of the sound of the mule's cadence as they rode in the back of the primitive wagon and rattled down the back streets of Charleston. The feeling of swaying in the wagon came back to her, and Christine remembered the anxieties of the long night.

Every block of the city presented more hazards for Christine and her mother as they enacted their new roles of poor sharecroppers run off the land by the War. Union soldiers freely looted whatever building they chose and set many on fire. Several times they stopped the wagon to see if it carried anything of value, but the apparent poverty of the old couple made them uninteresting. To young Christine, the flames of the raging fires seemed to shoot as high as the smoky sky, and she covered her ears against the screams of terror and the gunfire that echoed through the city.

The old mule plodded on; the wagon wheels clattered on the cobblestones but grew less noisy when they reached the dirt roads of the city's outskirts. The fires became a general glow behind them on the horizon. Christine's heart leapt with joy when her mother moaned and slowly regained consciousness. The old woman tried to make the man stop the wagon so she could help Christine's mother, but he insisted that they were not yet safe and must keep moving. It was left to young Christine to calm her mother and keep her quiet.

When dawn finally came, the old man drove the wagon off the road into the woods and hid them from marauding bands of armed men—some of them soldiers, some deserters. Fearful that a campfire would make them visible, he allowed the old woman to make a fire just long enough to brew coffee and make corn pone, and then he kicked dirt over the coals and put the fire out.

Christine helped her mother settle at the base of a spreading live oak and held a tin cup of coffee to her lips. Her mother drank eagerly and ate the corn pone the woman brought her on a tin plate.

Christine drank some water but had no appetite for the tasteless corn pone.

"You just put that plate of corn pone over there on that small rock and save it for later," the old woman told her. "You're gonna get hungry eventually and be mighty glad to have it."

Christine doubted she could ever eat the stuff, but she did as she was told.

As soon as the man had eaten, he lay down under the wagon and fell asleep. The old woman went in search of a creek, and when she returned, she brought a bucket of water and some rags to Christine's mother.

"We best wash that cut on your head," she said, "and them scrapes on your arms."

"Thank you for your kindness." Christine's mother patted the woman's arm. "We owe you our lives."

The old woman nodded and began rolling up the sleeves of the homespun dress Christine's mother wore.

Christine gasped when she saw that her mother's arms and hands were black and blue and covered with cuts.

"Shhh," her mother soothed her. "They are just bruises and scrapes I got stumbling around in the dark, banging on doors. They will heal."

Christine watched as the old woman gently washed the cut on her mother's head, then handed the cloth to Christine. "You wash your mama's arms and hands. I got some ointment for her head in the wagon."

"Does she know who we are?" Christine's mother whispered after the woman had stumbled off. "When I was unconscious, what did they say?"

"She just kept telling the man to save us. I don't think she knows about Father."

"Do you know who they are?"

"Her name is Anna Clayton. His name is Ira. Only I have to call them Grandma and Grandpa. That's what she said."

"Do as she said, darling. She is trying to protect us. Now, I want you to remember this: from now on, our last name is not Gibbes. It is Boyd."

"Like our cousins?"

"Yes, and we are going to try to get to the Boyd plantation. The Boyds will take us in and protect us because we are family."

"But that's a long way from Charleston." Christine's voice rose.

"Which is exactly why it will be safer for us. Shhh. Here she comes. Remember, you are a Boyd."

"Put this here ointment on your mama's cuts," the old woman ordered Christine as she squatted next to them. "I got other things to do while Ira's sleeping."

Much to Christine's amazement the old woman pulled a pearl necklace and earrings from her own pocket and began to rip open the hem of Christine's borrowed, homespun dress.

"No matter what happens, don't you be telling nobody 'bout what I'm doing," she ordered as she slipped the pearls into the hem of Christine's dress and began to stitch it up. "You understand, honey? Don't tell nobody." She pointed to her sleeping husband.

"What is she doing?" Christine asked her mother.

Her mother's eyes filled with tears. "She is protecting us. She knows the pearls are all we have of value." Christine's mother reached over and patted the old woman's cheek. "Thank you."

"Where you want to go?"

"To the Boyd plantation in Dorchester County."

"That's a far piece. He ain't gonna like that one bit."

"I am Julia Boyd. If you can help us get to the Boyd Plantation, I am sure my husband's family will reward you."

The old woman sewed in silence. When she had finished, she bit off the thread, stuck the needle into a thick piece of cloth, pocketed it and looked Christine's mother in the face.

"We can use the money, that's for certain, Miz Boyd, but we done got our reward." The old woman looked up at the sky, then heaved herself to her feet. "You rest yourself now. We're gonna have a long night."

Christine watched the woman stumble away, then asked, "Mother, what does she mean that she has gotten her reward? We have not given her any money or anything."

Her mother pulled her into her arms. "She means that her reward comes from God."

"From God?"

"In the Bible, Jesus tells us that when we help the least of our brethren, then we are helping Him. Remember? We've read the story many times."

"Is it the story about giving poor people food and visiting them when they are sick, like we used to do in Charleston?"

"Yes, darling, that is the one. Jesus said, 'When you did it for the least of these, you did it for me.'"

"Who are the 'least'?"

"The poorest. Those who are the most helpless."

"Are we the poorest now?"

"We are, and we aren't." Christine's mother hugged her. "You see, right now we are the 'least' for this woman. We have nothing, and this poor woman is sharing what she has with us."

"She is doing what Jesus said to do?"

"She is, and she knows her reward will come from God. But even though we are in a difficult situation, there are people who have even less than we do."

"There are? Who?"

"People who do not have a woman like this woman helping them. People who are helpless and do not have family or friends to help them."

Christine settled against her mother and thought about her words.

"Mother, if I promise Jesus I will always help the 'least,' will He help us get to Boyd Plantation?"

Christine's mother stroked her head. "He will help us no matter what you do, honey. You do not have to strike a bargain with God. He loves you."

"Then why do we help the 'least'?"

"Because we love God."

"Oh-h-h." Christine began to understand. "We help people because we love Jesus, and He loves the poor."

"That is right, darling. Now, I want you to eat some of that corn pone and then lie down on a bed of leaves and sleep. We need to rest while we can. We have a long and difficult journey ahead of us."

Christine picked up the tin plate, moved a few feet away from her mother, but carefully placed the plate on the leaves without eating. Instead, she lay on her back with her hands beneath her head propping it up a bit. She stared up into the canopy of the ancient live oak and noticed how its thick limbs gracefully swept down and out, creating a protected world for the creatures who lived there. Many types of birds swooped around in that world, and she even spotted several nests. Squirrels stared down at her, and apparently deciding she was no threat, began to chase each other. She heard the tapping of a woodpecker searching for its food in the bark of the tree.

Somehow, staring up into that gigantic tree made it easy for Christine to talk to God. She kept her voice soft so she would not wake her mother, but she had no doubt that God could hear her.

"Dear God, I know I'm little, but I want You to know that I promise to help poor people just like Jesus said to. You do not have to give me anything special. I will just help them because Jesus loves them. Amen." She turned over on her side, closed her eyes, and tried to sleep. Long, long minutes passed, and she felt fidgety. Finally, she gave up, turned onto her back again, and stared up into the tree. She watched the birds and squirrels going about their business, happily coexisting in the beautiful, safe world of the live oak. She thought about the frightening days she had experienced in Charleston and especially about the horrors of the night before. Here in the quiet of the woods, with the sun dappling through the live oak, it was almost impossible for her to believe that just hours before she had been running through the streets of a burning city with gunshots and screams all around her. *Why do people act like that? Why do they hate each other so much?* None of it made sense to her.

She remembered the moment she had first seen Grandma Anna and how the old woman had opened her arms and held her close to comfort her. She remembered the times that soldiers had stopped them as they exited the city and how Grandpa Ira had just patiently put up with whatever he had to, in order to keep them safe and moving out of the city. Once, some soldiers had even pulled him out of the wagon and slapped him to the ground. Christine had been terrified, but Grandpa Ira just lay there listening to all the ugly, mean words the soldiers heaped on him. Finally, the men had kicked him, mounted their horses and ridden away.

What if the next time the soldiers kill him? That thought made Christine shudder, and she focused on the birds so she wouldn't think about it anymore. She spotted a large, yellow butterfly gliding around a lower branch of the tree, and her worried mind relaxed. Slowly, slowly it circled and flitted through the limbs, and Christine began to wish it would come light on her. She lay very still, following the butterfly with her eyes until it lit on a low branch that swooped almost to the ground not far away from her. She squinted and tried hard to see its markings, but instead she saw a pair of dark eyes looking back at her.

Christine drew in her breath, and with her mouth still hanging open in surprise, slowly sat up and squinted harder. The dark eyes emerged from the foliage, and she realized that they were part of a dark-brown face, the face of a boy not much bigger than she was. Christine followed the boy's eyes as they darted first to the wagon with the sleeping couple under it, to her sleeping mother, back to Christine, and finally to the plate of corn pone lying on the rock next to her.

Christine's heart thumped wildly. She felt both afraid of the strange boy and concerned about him. She realized she had been presented with someone who was even more "least" than she was. She and her mother might be running away from the Yankee soldiers, but this boy's situation was worse. He had no place to run to. There was no Boyd Plantation waiting to take him in. Christine swallowed hard, drew in a deep breath to build up her courage, reached for the tin plate, and stood.

She inched toward the boy holding out the plate to him. When she had almost reached him, he lunged for the plate, turned and disappeared. Christine sank to the leaf-padded ground and struggled to catch her breath. The whole episode had happened so fast she could hardly believe it had happened at all. She was trembling with fear, but she knew she had kept her promise to God. She had helped the "least." It had been hard to do, but she had done it, and a tiny new joy had been born in her. When she could breathe normally, she crept back to her mother's side, lay down, and fell asleep.

Christine awakened some hours later to hear Grandpa Ira arguing with Grandma Anna about whether to head due west or to take Christine and her mother to Boyd Plantation. Christine crawled closer so she could hear better.

"The Lord put Miz Boyd and her little girl in our path, Ira, and we gotta help them," Grandma Anna insisted.

"I ain't trying to be cruel, woman. I'm just being practical. There ain't nothing left for us in South Carolina. We gotta head west."

"If you're just being practical, then you oughta want to take Miz Boyd to Boyd Plantation. They'll likely reward us for saving their kinfolk."

Grandpa Ira raised his voice. "Ain't likely no money left at Boyd Plantation. More likely the house is burnt to the ground."

Grandma Anna crossed her arms. "Ain't no way of knowing that without going there, and you know it."

"I know the Yankees been burning down plantation houses all over South Carolina!"

"Ira, you're a godly man, and we both know what you're gonna do, so why are we wasting time arguing 'bout it?"

Ira threw his hands in the air and sighed loudly. "I give up! You're the most confounded stubborn woman I ever met."

"I ain't just being stubborn."

Grandpa Ira walked to her side. "That little girl reminds you of our Nelly, don't she?"

Grandma Anna stared at the sky. "Nobody helped our Nelly get home."

Grandpa Ira lumbered over to Grandma Anna and took her in his arms. "The Lord gives and the Lord takes away. Ain't that what we agreed to stand on?"

The woman fiercely wiped her cheeks. "He gave us these two last night."

The old man shook his head. "When am I gonna learn that there ain't no point arguing with you, Anna? You done prayed on it and made up your mind."

She smiled up at him. "Don't you go laying this on me, old man. Your heart's a good one, and God's already convicted you, too."

"Well, when dark comes, I figure we'll head toward Dorchester County and hope the Yankees don't get there 'fore us."

"I've got a feeling 'bout this, Ira. That Boyd plantation will still be standing. You'll see."

Christine was so relieved she burst into tears. She hurried back to the base of the tree to tell her mother, but she stopped short when she saw her tin plate lying on the rock close to where she had been sleeping. It was empty.

The sun outside the church rose just high enough to send its rays through a vivid yellow pane in the stained glass window and into Christine's eyes. She squeezed them shut against the uncomfortable glare and returned her thoughts to the present.

"Goodness me!" she exclaimed to the empty sanctuary. "I seem to be determined to wander in the past instead of finishing the morning's errands. I must take control of my mind."

She rose and slowly walked the perimeter of the sanctuary, pausing to look at each of the stunning windows. *All this beauty—the gift of an immigrant.* She thought of the new Czech and German immigrants who had settled nearby recently. What gifts might they have to offer Riverford? Yet the town had already decided to reject them. To squeeze whatever cheap labor out of them it could and then to push them away. *How foolish! How wrong.*

She thought of her anger over Fanny Sharp's personal jabs at her. "Forgive me, Lord. What do such things matter? I need Your approval alone."

She remembered her morning's visit into the slums: the blank stares of the skinny, hungry children; the despondent despair of the adults. "Oh, that I could help some of them! I did make You that promise so long ago, Lord. I haven't forgotten. There are just so many who need help, and it is so easy to become overwhelmed!"

She had reached the piano. "Before I can do any more, I must keep my promise to the rector." She settled on the bench and began to play, softly singing the first stanza of her favorite hymn.

"Be though my vision, O Lord of my heart;

Naught be all else to me save that Thou art;

Thou my best thought, by day or by night.

Waking or sleeping, Thy presence my light."

She paused, slumped her fingers onto the keyboard, and bowed her head in prayer.

"This is the way, isn't it, Lord? I simply keep my eyes on You, and You will show me not only those who need my help, but also how to encourage others in the town to help its poorer citizens and its neighbors on the farms. I am not meant to do it all myself."

Where there is hatred, let me sow love; where there is despair, hope.

Christine smiled as the words of St. Francis again floated through her mind. "My job is simply to sow seeds. Tradition changes when someone steps out and dares to make changes. I am the wife of Riverford's most prominent citizen. How much easier it is for me to step out and sow those much-needed seeds. Surely the others will follow, and in time we will have a great harvest."

Content now, she turned her attention back to testing the piano for the rector.

Chapter Six

The relentless sun had completely dried their clothes, and new rivulets of perspiration dribbled down their backs and faces by the time Jana and Sally reached the outskirts of the town. Hunger had also overtaken them; Jana's empty stomach cramped, and she began to feel light headed again. Sally's slowed, unsteady step told her that the child also needed food.

The first house on the edge of town was just a small cottage in much need of repair. It was unlikely the tenants had a dime to spare, but Jana decided she couldn't afford to be choosy. She walked around to the back and knocked on the door. The woman who answered was dressed no better than she and laughed at Jana's request for work.

"Are you crazy?" she demanded. "Just look at this place. I ain't got no money to hire no help."

"Maybe we could work for food...."

"Ain't got no food to spare either. I got my own family to feed. You get yourself off my property and quit wasting my time." She turned her back and walked away.

"Wait!" Jana called after her. "Do you know of anyone who does need help?"

The woman roared with sarcastic laughter, then surprised Jana by whirling around and charging toward her. "Look at me!" she demanded. "Do I like look someone the quality would even talk to? They got their noses so high in the air it ain't likely they ever even seen the likes of me."

The woman turned and stalked back into the shadows of the cottage.

Jana took Sally's hand. "Come on, honey. She's right. We got to go to the richer part of town."

They walked seven blocks toward the center of the town. As the size of the houses increased, Jana's hopes rose in spite of a return of her dizziness. Surely these people needed help, and certainly they had the money to pay a good worker. The eighth block held sizable houses with well-maintained yards, and there was a church on one side of the street. Jana doubted her ability to walk another block, so she chose one of the houses at random, a house with tall holly hedges lining the sidewalk and shielding the immaculate, front garden. Her hand shook as she opened the iron gate, and she swayed a bit as she walked up the sidewalk. The house looked like a serene haven to Jana. Its porch swept across the front and around both sides, inviting one into the coolness of its shade and the comfort of its wicker furniture. In spite of her heroic efforts to overcome her lightheaded feeing, Jana staggered a bit as she approached the front porch.

"What are you doing in my yard?" A well-dressed woman stepped out of the shadows of the porch.

"Good morning, ma'am." Jana struggled to stand up straight. "I'm looking for work. I can wash clothes or scrub floors or—"

"Do you actually think I'd hire one of your kind?"

"I'm a hard worker, ma'am, and—"

"If you were such a hard worker, you wouldn't be here begging for work. You'd be out on whatever farm you obviously came from, working right this minute!"

"My husband and my little boys have been picking cotton since before dawn, ma'am, but we won't get paid until the crop is in. I need to earn some money—or some food, even—right now. I have three little boys—"

"I don't care to know one thing about your family. I didn't choose to have all those children. I declare! I believe you sharecroppers breed like rabbits or something."

"Ma'am, my children are hungry. My little girl here—"

"Why can't you people understand? We don't want your kind here. I'd hire a colored before I'd hire the likes of you. Go back to where you came from!"

"We're just trying to provide for our children. Just like you—"

"How dare you say such a thing to me?" The woman drew herself up and stuck her chin in the air. "You're nothing like me! You're a foreigner."

Jana felt her head sinking. "Ma'am, do you think you could give us some water?"

"I have no intention of doing one thing that will encourage the likes of you to invade this town. Now you get on your way, or I'll send for the sheriff."

Jana felt Sally tugging on her hand, so she turned and stumbled down the sidewalk. Across the street she saw a sycamore tree that promised shade. When they had crossed the street, she sank down on the curb, and through blurring vision, studied Sally's tomato-red face. Cicadas screeched from the limbs of the tree as it dropped its brown, curled-edged, exhausted leaves around her. She ducked her head between her knees in a last-ditch effort to stop herself from passing out. *I can't faint. I can't! What will happen to Sally?*

Sally slumped down beside her, and panic radiated through Jana when she realized the child was unconscious.

"Sally!" Jana jerked the child into her lap and frantically looked up and down the street for help. Not a single person was visible, but to Jana's amazement she heard the sound of a piano playing. Beautiful notes lilted around her. *Where are they coming from? Am I dying?* The shock of that thought sent a bolt of terror through her. *What will happen to Sally if I die?* She scooped the child up, and overcoming her own shakiness through sheer willpower, managed to stand. The volume of the music increased, and Jana realized it was coming from the church. *Someone is in the church! If only I can carry Sally that far.* She staggered forward, struggling for each step, encouraged onward by the music until she reached the ornately carved oak doors of the church. Utterly spent, she turned and threw her back again the doors. They gave way, and she tumbled into the shadowy foyer of the church. Straight ahead of her a white marble fount gleamed, and Jana saw water in it.

She staggered forward and, utilizing her last strength, sat Sally in the water before she slipped into darkness, falling, falling.

Chapter Seven

The tragedies of Christine's childhood, as well as the upsetting events of the morning, drifted away as she played the piano. Light flooded through the jewel tones of the stained glass windows, creating a collage of ethereal light on the open top of the gleaming cherry grand piano. Christine moved from simple hymns, to lively Mozart, to a swaying Strauss waltz. She now existed in another world, a world where the heart strings were wrung not by human suffering or meanness of spirit, but instead by sheer flights of beauty. She began to play a beloved nocturne of Chopin's. The music began gently, then slowly increased in volume and intensity. Christine's heart was engaged completely, lifting on the ascending notes of the treble, but steadied by the repetitive beat of the bass. She had just reached the climax of the piece when she heard a child scream.

Jerked back into the confines of the church building, Christine's fingers sprang off the keyboard and hung in the air. *I must have imagined it.*

The child screamed again. "Mama, Mama!"

Christine jumped from the piano stool, raced up the aisle to the back of the sanctuary, and burst through the double doors into the entry. She was shocked to see a woman crumpled at the base of the baptismal font and a girl of six or seven crouched by her side screaming. "Don't leave me, Mama! Wake up!"

Christine raced to the woman's side, flung herself to her knees beside the still body, and lifted the woman's head in her hands. She was scorching hot to the touch.

The child's petrified eyes met Christine's, and she cried out. "Help her! She's dying!"

Water! Christine remembered the pitcher of water left by the rector. She scrambled on her hands and knees, grabbed the heavy silver pitcher, and lugged it back to the woman's side. Slowly she poured the cool water through the woman's hair, using her hand to bath the woman's face and neck.

"Get one of those paper fans out of the basket over there and fan her head," she ordered the child. The girl jumped up, swayed for a moment, then staggered to the basket. When she returned, she fell to her knees and fanned her mother furiously.

"Good girl," Christine encouraged. "Just keep fanning."

Christine opened the woman's blouse and loosened her skirt, then dribbled water on the woman's neck and chest. Soon the pitcher was empty, and the woman was still unconscious. The little girl dropped the fan and began to wail.

Christine stood, slipped off her petticoat, and dunked it in the baptismal font.

"Keep fanning her," she insisted as she wrapped the woman's head and neck in the sodden petticoat and gently slapped her cheeks.

The woman moaned.

"She is regaining consciousness." At Christine's words, the little girl began sobbing hysterically and latched on to her mother's shoulders.

"No, no." Christine pulled the desperate child away. "She must have air. Keep fanning her."

"Sally...Sally," the woman murmured.

"I'm here, Mama. I'm here." The girl fanned more vigorously.

"That's the way," Christine said. "She is going to be just fine."

Suddenly a slice of glaring light cut across the shadows of the foyer as the entry door opened and Mrs. Sharp rushed in, with Mrs. Drift on her heel.

"What in the name of—Mrs. Boyd, are you all right?" Mrs. Sharp demanded. "The moment we saw that woman come in the church, we came immediately to rescue you."

"Oh dear, dear Christine, I pray you have not been harmed by this—this...." Clementine Drift's words petered out as she examined the woman lying on the floor. She gasped. "Why, Fanny, this is the very woman who accosted us on your front porch. One of those immigrants!"

Mrs. Sharp shook her head angrily. "Everywhere they go, trouble is sure to follow. Why, just look at this terrible mess she has made... and in the church no less!"

"We must send for help, for the sheriff," Mrs. Drift's voice rose in pitch. "We can't allow dangerous people like this to roam around the town."

"No, please." The woman struggled to sit up but slumped backward. Christine caught her in her arms, gently laid her back on the stone floor, and stroked her head. "Please don't let them—"

"Everything is going to be fine," Christine soothed her. "There will be no trouble, I promise."

"There most certainly will be trouble!" Mrs. Sharp exclaimed.

"Mama was just trying to get work," the little girl blurted out. "Mr. Lynch won't pay Pa his wages, and we don't have any food." She jumped to her feet and turned on Fanny Sharp. "She just wants to work, but you wouldn't even listen!"

"Why you impudent piece of trash!" Fanny Sharp lashed back. "You ought to be whipped within an inch of your life."

Christine's memory of her flight from Charleston with her mother collided with the plight of the woman lying before her, and she saw the truth—a woman trying to save her daughter and those who could help her resolutely turning away. She had lived this story. She looked into the frightened eyes of the girl called Sally, and a thunderbolt of truth shook her. *I was once that helpless child, but I am not a helpless child anymore!*

Christine sprang to her feet. "That is enough, Fanny! Your remarks are reprehensible. This poor woman was so overheated she collapsed, and it is clear to me that you could have prevented that."

"Taking care of the likes of women like that is not my responsibility!"

"Isn't it? We are either Christians, or we are not Christians!"

Fanny Sharp glared at Christine, but Clementine Drift stared at the floor and muttered, "I don't know what to think about all this."

"There will be plenty of time to think later," Christine answered. "Right now, you need to act. This woman and her child need water and food. I know I can depend on you, Mrs. Drift, to hurry home and bring those necessities back."

Mrs. Sharp grabbed Mrs. Drift's arm, "Don't you dare do such a thing, Clementine!"

She turned her vehemence on Christine. "Can't you see that if you crack open the door to this town, a horde of those immigrants will descend on us?"

"Would that be such a bad thing?"

"Yes, it would! Why, Riverford would be—would be—"

"Given the opportunity to act Christ like," Christine finished the furious woman's sentence.

"Ruined! I was going to say 'ruined,'" Mrs. Sharp retorted.

"You are worrying about the future, Fanny, when it is our job to live in the present and help those whom God puts in our path."

"Well, I refuse to be a part of this!" Mrs. Sharp shouted at her. "I have my reputation to consider." Her mouth twisted, and her tone became a taunt. "And you—you are supposed to be such a high and mighty lady sent to us from Charleston to show us how to live. Well, if you ask me, Mrs. Boyd—"

"I do *not* ask you!" Christine raised her voice and was immediately astounded to hear her anger ricocheting off the stone walls. *Dear Lord, what is happening to me? This is not supposed to be about me.* She gritted her teeth and slowly inhaled, exerting her willpower to rein in the anger that threatened to blur her focus. "I do not *need* to ask you, Fanny, because I have heard the Scriptures from my earliest years. So ... have ... you. That is why I know that you will rethink your position and I can *count on* you to send a message to my husband while Mrs. Drift gathers water and food."

Mrs. Sharp's mouth sprang open, ready to refuse.

"She's right, Fanny!" Mrs. Drift began to cry. "God forgive us. She is right."

"Go, go now, Clementine," Christine urged. "These people need help now."

Mrs. Drift nodded and hurried to the door.

Mrs. Sharp sighed in exasperation. "You are hopeless, Mrs. Boyd. I'll send the note to your husband, the poor man. Maybe he can make you see the truth." She turned to leave, but looking back over her shoulder, snapped. "You are young, Christine Boyd. Time will teach you the error of your ways."

"Then may God end my life this moment."

Mrs. Sharp's eyes filled with fury, but she pursed her lips and bolted for the door. Christine sank to her knees before the woman and the little girl. "I am so sorry you had to hear that. Please forgive us."

The woman clutched her arm. "Don't let her send for the sheriff. If he arrests my husband—"

"Don't worry about that. I promise you that you are safe now, and we are going to help you." She patted the woman's shoulder. "What is your name?"

"Jana Novak, and this is my girl, Sally."

Christine smiled at the child. "You are a very brave little girl, Sally. Now why don't we help your mother sit up."

Sally rushed to her mother's side, and they pulled Jana up to a sitting position.

"How do you feel?" Christine anxiously hovered over her. "Are you dizzy?"

"Not too much."

"Do you think you can stand? If you can, Sally and I will support you and help you to a pew inside the sanctuary."

"Oh, I could never go in there! I'm too dirty and wet. Besides, people like me don't belong in fine places like that."

Stinging tears sprang into Christine's eyes, and she had to study the stained glass window a moment to regain her composure. "You are quite wrong," she finally managed to say. "You belong in there more than anyone. Let us see if you can stand."

It was a struggle, but with Sally's help, Christine managed to help Jana stand, and despite her dizziness, to walk through the sanctuary door and sit on the back pew.

"Lay down, Mama," Sally urged as she bent to lift her mother's feet.

"No, honey, no. This is good enough. I can't be putting my dirty boots on that fancy velvet cushion."

"Mrs. Drift will be back any minute with water and food," Christine said, "so if you do feel well enough to sit up—"

"I do. And I'll be less dizzy if I stay upright."

Christine sat down beside her. "Well then, while we wait, why don't you tell me about your circumstances so we can make a plan."

Jana looked down at her rough hands resting on her stained, wet skirt.

"Please," Christine encouraged her.

"I figure Sally summed it up right well. We're sharecroppers, working for Mr. Lynch. He ain't paid my husband since last spring, and we ain't got any food left." She looked directly into Christine's eyes. "I got three hungry little boys back at the farm working in the fields, and then there's Sally. It just came over me this morning that we weren't gonna make it. That's when I decided to come to town to find work."

Christine patted Jana's hands. "You did the right thing."

"Kazimir—that's my husband—is mighty proud, and he didn't want me to come, but I had to. I couldn't let my children go hungry another day."

Clementine Drift hurried through the door lugging a full shopping basket. "I just grabbed everything I saw," she exclaimed as she set the basket down. "I've got bread and preserves. Some apples. And I threw some slices of ham in."

"Let us start with just some water for Mrs. Novak," Christine suggested, but when she saw Sally's eyes light up, she added. "Give Sally some food with her water."

Sally vehemently shook her head. "I won't eat 'till Mama eats."

"Oh, but you must eat right away," Mrs. Drift insisted. "Why, a child needs food to grow. No child should ever go without—" Her words ground to a halt, and her lips quivered as her eyes filled with tears.

Christine studied Clementine's face. *She's torn...trying to make a choice.*

"I'm so ashamed, Christine," Mrs. Drift blurted out. "Please, forgive me."

"You do not need *my* forgiveness."

"Yes, I do! Oh, Christine. Fanny sent me over with this food so you would just feed them and get rid of them."

Christine jumped up. "Did she send a message to my husband?"

Clementine's tears overflowed her eyes. "No."

Fury shot through Christine. She wanted to march out of the church, find Fanny Sharp and cover her with scathing words. Lacking that possibility, she wanted to grab Clementine and shake her. Instead she turned away from all of them and scanned the church, her eyes flitting from window to window. *Be Thou my vision, Lord! Please. Help me control my mind, control my tongue.* It came to her that this morning's battle was about more than caring for Jana and Sally. It was about Clementine and yes, even about Fanny. She bowed her head into her hands. *Help me, Lord! Help me extinguish my anger. Make me an instrument of Thy peace.*

When she turned back, she had regained control of herself. She looked into Clementine's eyes and asked quietly, "What are *you* going to do about it?"

Clementine looked down at Sally, who lifted her head and boldly met the woman's eyes. Decision made, Clementine brusquely swiped the tears from her cheeks. "I'll send my boy Tommy. He can run like the wind. We'll have help here in no time." She turned on her heel and hurried from the sanctuary.

"Thank you, Lord." Jana's voice was weak.

Christine reached down and squeezed Jana's shoulder. "Yes indeed. I think He has saved more than you and Sally this morning. I know He has saved me." She turned her attention to the little girl. "Dig into that basket, Sally, and pass us some water for your mother."

"You go ahead and eat, Sally girl," Jana insisted. "I'll just have a good drink of water and then I'll be ready for some of that bread."

The child did as she had been told, and Christine leaned over Jana focusing on her needs, encouraging her to sip water slowly, and finally to eat some bread. When she looked up again, she saw that Sally had moved away from the pew and was reaching up and tracing her finger around the pieces of colored glass in the lower section of the nearest window.

"That is a beautiful window, isn't it?" Christine tried to strike up a conversation with the child.

"I know this Bible story. Mama read it to me."

"It is one of my favorite stories," Christine said, "and that window—"

Sally turned abruptly and faced her. "Why doesn't Jesus give us food? He gave food to all those people in the Bible story. Why doesn't He help us too?"

Christine's heart lurched. She went and knelt before Sally. "Jesus expects us—people like me—to do that for you. Jesus has not failed you, Sally. I have. This town has. Now that Jesus is no longer on earth, we are supposed to be his hands and feet. We are supposed to help the people He would help if He was still physically here."

The child stared directly into Christine's eyes. "Why don't you?"

"We are selfish."

Sally nodded.

"But we are going to change," Christine promised. "It will take time, but—"

Sally's hands shot up and clenched into tiny fists of desperation. "But we are hungry now! We can't wait!"

"Sally!" Jana exclaimed. "Watch your manners. You mustn't say things like that—"

"I don't care! When I'm grown up, I'm going to help poor people."

Christine grabbed the child's hands and smiled at her through tears. "I believe you will, Sally. I know you will."

"Christine! Christine, where are you?" A man's voice boomed out in the foyer.

"It is Richard!" Christine exclaimed as she sprang up and hurried to the door. She found him staring at the mess next to the baptismal font. "I am so *glad* you have come."

"Are you all right, darling?" He hurried to her. "What has happened here?"

"I'm fine. A woman and her little girl came into the church and collapsed from heat and hunger. Come." She took his hand. "I'll introduce you to them, and we'll make a plan to help them."

"We will?"

"We will."

He smiled down at her. "I see. It's already decided. Well then, I guess you better tell me what you know."

"They are sharecroppers on Tom Lynch's land. Kazimir Novak is the man's name. There are four children and another on the way. Tom Lynch hasn't paid them since last spring."

Richard's face darkened. "I see."

"Richard, they need food right now. Heaven only knows what else they need."

"Okay. I understand. You gather your things, and I'll take you home and then—"

"No, I'll stay here with them. You go gather some supplies for them, and we'll take them back to the farm."

"Christine, there's no need for you to go way out there. Stay here now if you want, but I don't want you involved in whatever may be happening out on that land."

"Richard, I must go. I feel compelled to go. More is happening here than meets the eye."

"What do you mean?"

"I mean that Riverford must change its behavior toward people like these. You and I have been blessed with money and prominent social position. We must lead the way."

Richard looked deeply into his wife's eyes for a long, silent moment. "You have found a mission field, haven't you?"

She smiled and nodded. "At least it's not in China, darling."

He grinned. "Thank God for that because we'd be on our way to China instead of out to Lynch's land. Okay, here's what I'm going to do. You stay here, and I'll be back with a carriage, provisions for them, and a decent lunch for you."

"Tell Josie to make the boys—"

He waved her words away. "Josie can handle the boys. My goal is to get this done as efficiently as possible and get my wife back to the comfort of her home." He kissed her on the forehead. "I'll be back as soon as possible. You go sit down!"

As he turned to go, the door opened and Clementine Drift slipped through.

"I saw Mr. Boyd's buggy," she began hesitantly. "I just thought...well...you'll be needing a wagon, and I have one—"

"Good morning, Mrs. Drift," Richard bowed slightly. "I think the ladies will be more comfortable in our carriage. I'll be back with supplies as quickly as I can." He left.

Mrs. Drift approached Christine. "I want to do something more, Christine. I feel so bad...."

Christine smiled at her. "Let's not waste time on the past. We cannot change it. Why don't we simply chart a new and better future."

"Tell me what I can do."

"We must proceed cautiously. Mrs. Novak says her husband is too proud to accept help."

"But the children are suffering!"

"Exactly. And I know that if we ladies put our heads together, we can think of a way to help without injuring his pride. I'll know more after I actually see their circumstances."

Mrs. Drift's eyes widened as her mouth fell open. "You're going out there?"

"Yes, I am."

"But what will people think? I mean, you'll be going against tradition, and people...."

Christine's eyes twinkled. "Maybe we ladies need to learn to skirt tradition."

"Skirt it?"

"Yes. Skirt it. Don't defy it directly; just skirt around the edges and get things done that need to be done."

Mrs. Drift grinned. "I was thinking that Mrs. Novak probably needs some clothes for her family."

Christine nodded. "She has three little boys out there working in the fields."

"How old do you figure they are?"

"I don't know for sure, but I imagine they are close to Sally's age, a little older and a little younger."

"My Tommy's grown like a weed this year. I've got plenty of boy's things, but what about the little girl?"

"Yes. What about that remarkable little girl?" Christine intentionally waited for Mrs. Drift to come up with an answer.

Mrs. Drift slammed her hands onto her waist. "I'll just go to the neighbors!" She turned on her heel and headed toward the door. "Don't you worry; I'll find that girl something to wear." She stopped before exiting and turned back to Christine. "One other thing. Fanny Sharp and I will clean up the church. She doesn't know it yet, but she'll be glad to do it."

Christine laughed.

Chapter Eight

By early afternoon Christine was standing under the shade of the only tree in sight, staring down endless rows of cotton to a tumbledown shanty at the edge of the field. On her left, three little boys were gulping down sandwiches while Jana and Sally supervised. Richard was talking to Kazimir Novak, asking his advice about crops for his own land, and complimenting the man on his farming skills. No mention had been made of Jana's collapse. Instead, Richard had thanked Mr. Novak for allowing his wife to "help them out" that morning and acted as if Jana had earned the boxes of provisions they had brought.

Christine quietly withdrew to a place where she could better study the shanty. It was small, undoubtedly no more than one room. The roof had been badly patched and, no doubt, leaked like a sieve when it rained. She searched the hard, red, sun-baked clay around the shanty for a well, but found none. She concluded that most likely a stream nearby provided the family's only source of water for drinking or bathing. It was easy to visualize the necessity of Jana or the little children lugging heavy buckets of water back to the shanty. And, no doubt, Jana beat their clothes clean on the rocks that surrounded the stream. Christine thought of her own little boys, now napping on the sleeping porch under the watchful eyes of Josie after having enjoyed a morning of play and a nutritious dinner. The contrast was painful.

The stone chimney of the shanty lay in a heap at one end of the building. *How do they cook? How will they keep warm this winter?* She scanned the yard again and found a fire pit. A vivid picture of Jana's trying to cook outdoors in the dead of winter came to Christine's mind. Blustery, freezing wind. Sleet threatening to extinguish the fire. And where would the children be while they waited for their meager meal? Huddled together, no doubt, in the only dry corner of the shanty. In spite of the sweltering September heat swirling around her, Christine shivered. She looked at Jana sitting at the base of the tree with three hungry boys snatching at the food she held out. She saw the swelling under Jana's skirt; the new baby would come in winter. *It will take a miracle to save it, and Jana might not survive either. Then what will happen to the children?*

A wave of anxiety washed over Christine and turned her stomach. She abruptly looked away from the shanty, from her painful insight into the reality of the Novak family's daily lives. When she did, she discovered that Sally was staring at her. The little girl's earnest, questioning face—far too thin and far too old for a child—jolted Christine. A battle between grief and fury erupted in Christine's tender heart. She swallowed hard, forcing back the strong emotions that threatened to debilitate her. *No! I must act. I cannot—I will not leave them in this situation!*

Christine realized that Richard was ending their visit. She watched in amazement as he offered Kazimir Novak his hand and wished him well. Was he really simply going to leave? When he came to her side and offered her his arm, she refused it.

"We cannot leave them like this, Richard," she whispered.

"We can't do anything else at the moment."

"But they will just go back out in that blazing sun. Jana will collapse again! I must at least offer her a job."

"No." Richard's voice was firm. "Her husband will never allow it. We must think of another way. Now, go say your good-byes."

Christine looked deep into her beloved husband's eyes and saw the veiled compassion that was so typical of him. Her confidence returned. She walked to the base of the tree, listened to Jana's words of gratitude, and said her own good-byes. In a day filled with great difficulties, leaving Jana, Sally, and the boys behind was the hardest thing she had had to do because she knew what lay ahead of them that afternoon. After they had picked cotton in the sizzling sun until dark, they would limp back to the shanty and sink into exhausted sleep. Christine's only comfort was the knowledge that they would not go to sleep hungry that night.

Christine patiently held her tongue as she and Richard traveled through the heat of the afternoon. Richard had said that they must "think of another way," and she assumed he was pondering the possibilities, but when he spoke, it was not about the Novaks.

"When you get home, Christine, promise me you will take a cool bath and lie down for the rest of the afternoon. This day has been far too strenuous for you."

Christine's patience evaporated in an instant. "Richard! How can you think about my comfort or health after seeing what we have just seen?"

He sighed as he pulled out a handkerchief to wipe his sweating face. "That's why I didn't want you to come out here. I know how sensitive you are."

"Sensitive? Do you really think I am merely being too sensitive?"

He shook his head. "No, you are being your usual compassionate self."

"Richard, this is not about me. It is not about my feelings. It is about their need."

"My dear, this valley is full of such sharecroppers and their families. They all have similar struggles."

"If that is true, we should be ashamed. The whole town of Riverford should be ashamed."

"You can't rescue all the poor people in the valley, Christine."

"I know that, but God has brought this family to my attention. How can I turn my back on them now?"

He turned his head and looked into her face. "You can't. I know that because I know you. It is the little girl who moves you the most, isn't it?"

"How did you know?"

"I could see it in your eyes. It is the little girl and the mother's desperate attempts to save her. That dynamic is making you even more compassionate than you normally are. And that's saying a lot!"

They had reached the shadowy, relative coolness of the woods. Richard pulled back on the reins to stop the horses and turned to her. "Has their plight reminded you of your past?"

"Yes, it has. I have experienced some of the desperation they feel. Only a small part, really, and only for a short time when Mother and I had to flee Charleston. We had quite a harrowing experience. She had at first refused to leave when it was announced that the mayor would turn Charleston over to the Union forces. Our neighbors had only one day to gather up whatever they could take, find whatever horses and wagons they could find, and flee the city. General Sherman was coming, so they were eager to leave, but Mother refused to go. She was certain that Father was close by and would return to look for us."

Richard sighed. "And she was right. We weren't far away, but we were fighting for our lives and frantically trying to regroup the remaining troops."

"Mother said that Father would never abandon Charleston, and neither would she."

"She was a brave woman."

"And smart too. She knew we could not stay in the house. The city was already full of people who would gladly direct Union troops to the home of General Gibbes. So in the days before the surrender, she quietly moved us to an abandoned building. I was only nine; I do not remember all the details, but I certainly remember the fear."

"But your new location did not keep you safe."

"No. Someone—we never knew who—gave our location to the Union forces. The night after the surrender, the Yankees who had spent the day carousing and looting, came looking for us. We literally had to run for our lives through the back streets of Charleston."

"Why have you never told me about this?"

"Mother never wanted Father to know about it. She said he would never forgive himself."

"She was right about that. The General was frantic with worry about you two. I think he even thought of surrendering himself in order to protect you."

"I doubt that would have made any difference. Charleston had held off the Union forces for four years, and when they finally took the city, they were in no mood for generosity."

"I know, but believe me, a soldier's most difficult task is staying on the battlefield when he knows his family is in immediate danger. I shall be eternally grateful that those who remained behind with you helped you escape."

Christine turned her face away, bit her lips, and studied her hands tensely clasped in her lap.

"What is it?" Richard covered her hands with one of his and gently turned her face back where he could see it. "What are you not telling me?"

"It was twenty years ago. I don't know whether I should talk about it."

"Of course you should. It is clearly on your mind, and, I suspect, somehow tied to your strong feelings for the Novak family."

Christine sighed. "Richard, I have a confession to make."

"I'm listening, darling."

"My thoughts about those horrible days of my childhood did not begin when Jana and Sally showed up at the church. I had already been thinking about those days earlier that morning."

"And what prompted those thoughts?"

"I have been taking food across the railroad tracks into the colored section. I have been waiting until you left in the morning and walking down there."

"I know."

"You do?"

He pulled her close to him and put his arm around her shoulders. "My darling girl, do you really think the gossips of Riverford haven't been eager to bring your supposed misdeeds to my attention?"

"But you said nothing!"

"I said nothing because I know you have good intentions and I trust your good sense. But what have these charitable acts of yours got to do with the days after Charleston surrendered?"

"When Mother and I had to flee, it was the middle of the night. Fires blazed everywhere; the air was filled with smoke; gunshots rang out all around us, and we could hear the Union soldiers right behind us."

Richard shook his head angrily. "What a horrific experience for a little girl. Thank God your friends rescued you."

"That's what Mother allowed Father to believe, but that's not what happened. Our friends were long gone. And our few neighbors who were left would not risk helping us."

"What do you mean? No one in Charleston would help rescue the wife and daughter of a Confederate General?"

"They were afraid. After all, the soldiers were literally on our heels. To take us into their homes meant inevitable and immediate danger to their own families."

Richard furiously slapped the reins, and the horses moved forward again. "Then how did you get away? How did you get to my family's plantation?"

"An old sharecropper couple pulled Mother and me into an alley, hid us until the troops had ridden past and then disguised us as members of their family. We made a slow, difficult journey in their old wagon out of the city."

"I can't believe you have never told me this!"

"By the time Mother and I saw you again, you had endured your own hell in a Yankee prison. Father had been caught and sentenced to a long term in prison, and Mother said that he had borne enough and did not need the further burden of guilt."

"I was lucky. They were not very interested in a young lieutenant, but the General...." His face tightened, and Christine saw anger flash in his eyes. "Union prisons were anything but kind to Confederate officers."

"I know." Christine paused, then added, "Actually I don't know. None of us knows what Father suffered after he was taken prisoner."

"Obviously we have never known what you suffered either." He was silent for a few moments. "I think I now understand why you feel so strongly about the plight of that little girl and her mother. You remember what it feels like to be helpless and unwelcome."

"Yes, I remember those feelings, but I remember something even more important."

"What could that be?"

"That Mother and I were rescued by the poorest of people. Those who had nothing to give and everything to lose extended mercy to us. Richard, those sharecroppers were not headed toward Boyd Plantation, and they had nothing but corn pone to eat, but they shared what they had with us and delivered us to a place of safety."

"Thank God."

"Yes, thank God. I thanked Him then, but I did more than that. I promised God that I would help the needy He put in my path. I promised Him that I would never turn away from the helpless."

"That was a time of war, a time of immense upheaval and violence."

"Do you think these people are fighting any less of a war? Isn't fighting for survival the same no matter what the circumstances? Richard, I must keep my promise to God. I must help them. Jana and Sally did not stumble into St. Paul's by accident. It was no coincidence that I chose that hour to be there testing the new piano."

Richard held up his hand to stop her. "I surrender! We will help them, but I insist you leave the details to me." He reined in the horses as they approached the stable behind the house. "I want you to rest this afternoon."

"How can I rest knowing that Jana and those children are picking cotton out in the broiling sun?"

Richard jumped down from the carriage and reached up to help Christine down. When her feet touched the ground, he held her still in front of him.

"My darling wife, you have kept your promise to God. You have rescued Mrs. Novak and her daughter in their hour of greatest need. You have made me aware of the problem and quite sufficiently aroused my conscience, I assure you. What you must do now is trust me to continue your rescue efforts in realms where you have no power."

"What do you plan to do?"

"I have an idea, but I need to proceed cautiously. Mr. Novak is not going to accept charity."

"Even if his family is starving?"

"Not under any circumstances. But you don't need to worry about that. I'll figure something out. And if you start to doubt my abilities, just remember that God is on the job too."

Christine threw her arms around his neck and kissed him soundly.

Chapter Nine

Alone at last, Jana walked out onto the porch of the cabin they had just moved into and tried to take in the amazing events of the day. Long before dawn she had trudged out into a wealthy man's cotton field with her small children sleepily straggling along. After several hours of backbreaking labor in the killing sun, she had collapsed. Her physical breakdown had forced her to acknowledge the hopelessness of her family's situation and given her the courage to take the long, steamy walk into town. Once there, she had been rebuffed and demeaned, but then a miracle had occurred. There was no other word for it. It had been a miracle. At her most desperate moment God had brought Mrs. Boyd into her life, and the whole direction of her life and that of her children had turned upward.

Her family now had a fresh start on a bigger, better farm. And miracle of all miracles, their work could actually make the land theirs. She turned back and looked at the house. Inside, her children were fast asleep, and for the first time in months, their bellies were full. In spite of his exhaustion, her husband had had a fresh spring in his step as he walked toward their bedroom. Their bedroom! For the first time in their marriage they had a bedroom of their own and another for the children. She walked to the edge of the porch and rattled the loose porch railing. Tears of joy welled up in her eyes. *A porch! We have a porch to sit on.* She thought of the big, central room of the house with its working stone fireplace where she had fed her family half an hour ago. *Amazing!* She peered out into the dusk and traced the outline of the old barn, and her eyes traveled to the well. *No more lugging water from a creek.*

It was more than she could take in. How could she, who had wandered from shanty to shanty with a baby in her arms and one in her belly, with her toddlers holding on to her skirt as they struggled to follow—how could she have ever imagined this would come to her?

"Oh Lord, my God, You have heard my pleas and delivered me," she proclaimed to the skies above.

Fireflies began to glow across the hard-packed, red clay yard, a cooler breeze rattled the weary leaves of an old oak nearby. Dry leaves, their edges curled and brittle, played around her feet as she stepped onto the warped boards of the steps and walked away from the house. When she reached the oak, she turned and looked back. "Everything needs some fixing up," she murmured, "but it's gonna be ours one day. Ours!"

Her thoughts flew back to the late afternoon hours. Doggedly she and Kazimir had continued picking Mr. Lynch's cotton long after the children had collapsed under the only tree in the field. Drenched in her own sweat, her eyes stung as her numb fingers repeatedly plucked at the sharp cotton bolls. She had heard a wagon rattling along the rutted road, and when she stood to peer across the blinding white field, she saw that it was being driven by Mr. Boyd and was followed by a second wagon driven by another man. For a moment she thought she had become delusional in the heat, but then she noticed that Kazimir and the children stood watching as well. She began the long walk toward the tree where the wagons had stopped, but Kazimir reached it first. Jana watched as Mr. Boyd introduced her husband to the other man and launched into what appeared to be an energetic speech. As she drew near, she began to catch phrases on the breeze.

"I know it is asking you to sacrifice a great deal," Mr. Boyd was saying to Kazimir, "and certainly I have no right to ask a favor of you, but if you could just consider helping me out, I would be most grateful, and I promise I will make it worth your sacrifice."

"But why me?" Kazimir asked as Jana walked up.

"Because of your skills, Mr. Novak. I saw this afternoon what you have done with Tom Lynch's worthless piece of land. No one else has ever gotten a cotton crop out of this soil."

"Mighty fine cotton it is, too." The other man waved his hand around the field. "Never seen anything but weeds on this here land."

"Neither have I, Brock," Mr. Boyd agreed, then continued appealing to Kazimir. "And there is the matter of your integrity. I can't name another sharecropper who would honor his agreement for six months without receiving one penny of compensation. Clearly, you are a man of your word, the kind of man I want working for me."

Jana gasped. Mr. Boyd was offering Kazimir a job!

"In fact, that brings me to the very reason I need your help. As I said, not all sharecroppers have your integrity, and one of my farms has been abandoned by a man I trusted. A fine crop of cotton is just going to waste as we speak! Why, my overseer here, Mr. Brock, has been forced to hire some migrant black men to pick that cotton."

"And I ain't got time enough to stand over them. I gotta oversee all Mr. Boyd's lands. I can't be tied to that one farm day in and day out," Mr. Brock complained.

"Look, Mr. Novak," Mr. Boyd said, "I am a businessman, plain and simple. I have a fine piece of land covered with prime cotton and no one to run that farm for me. I need your help. I realize I am making a bold request, but here is my offer. If you and your family will move over there tonight, I will start paying you wages right now, and I will draw up an agreement that makes you a tenant farmer who is buying a percentage of the land every year you work it. It will take you about twenty years of hard work, but in time you will own that farm."

"I can't see how this is gonna benefit you, Mr. Boyd," Kazimir responded.

Mr. Boyd took a step closer. "Why, I am going to make a prime profit off that land every year for the next twenty years while you are working to buy it. I will be an old man by then and glad to be rid of it."

"And you want us to go now?"

"I do. I'd feel a lot better if you were there in the morning to oversee the picking of that cotton."

"But I've signed an agreement with Mr. Lynch—"

Mr. Brock laughed harshly. "You can just forget that! If he ain't paid you since last spring, he don't have no right to hold you."

"I don't know. ... I did sign a paper."

"You don't need to worry about Mr. Lynch causing you any legal trouble," Mr. Boyd assured Kazimir. "I own the bank, and I hold the mortgages on all his land. In fact, I think I can assure you that Tom Lynch will be paying you the back wages he owes you."

Jana held her breath as Kazimir stared at the ground and kicked at the dirt with the toe of his boot.

"What do you say, Mr. Novak? Will you help me out?" Mr. Boyd asked.

Kazimir looked up and nodded. "Yes, sir. I can see you sure need help."

Mr. Boyd held out his hand. Kazimir stood up taller and shook it vigorously, and Jana realized her face was drenched in tears.

"I am mighty grateful," Mr. Boyd declared. "I was hoping you would agree, so I brought a couple of wagons to help you move. I know your family has been working all day, so if it is too much trouble for you to move now, you can wait until tomorrow, but I will need you in my fields before dawn to oversee those pickers."

"We'll move now," Kazimir said.

And they had. They had simply walked off Mr. Lynch's field, packed up their meager belongings and moved a mile or so to their new home. During all that activity, Jana never worried a minute. She figured that no matter where they were going, it would be better than where they had been.

"And I was right!" Jana exclaimed as she stared back at her new home. She tilted her head and caught the wafting scent of wild honeysuckle. "I'm gonna make me a garden. Food for my family and flowers for me." She lifted her scarred, sore-covered hand and pointed back to the porch. "I'm gonna put my flowers right there, right next to the porch so I can see them from the window. I'm gonna have a rocking chair, and I'm gonna sit and look at my flowers and watch dusk fall."

"What you pointing at, Mama?" Sally emerged from the deepening shadows of the porch.

"At our flower garden, baby girl."

Sally cocked her head and lowered her eyebrows, then suddenly a smile of understanding softened her face. She raced down the few steps and out to her mother's side. "Are you really gonna plant a flower garden?"

"I sure am."

"A real flower garden like the ones we saw in town?"

Jana smiled down at her daughter's face, which had grown more youthful the moment they had arrived at their new home. "Not just like the ones we saw in town. It's gonna be ours, yours and mine, whatever we choose to plant."

Sally grabbed her mother's arm. "Where's it gonna be, Mama? Where's it gonna be?"

"Right there." Jana pointed at the porch. "We're gonna plant flowers all across the front of the porch. That way we can see them whether we're coming or going."

"And we can see them from the kitchen window," Sally added. "Oh, Mama, just think, we got a kitchen table now and even a good fireplace."

"My children won't be cold this winter."

"And you can cook inside!"

Jana laughed at Sally's enthusiasm. "I'll tell you a secret, honey."

"What?"

"One of these days we're gonna have us a real stove to cook on and one of those fancy pumps that brings water right into the kitchen."

"We are?"

"We are. But first we're gonna scrub this house from top to bottom. Tomorrow you and I are gonna make it shine. And then we're gonna take some of those provisions Mr. Boyd brought, and we're gonna cook a big dinner for your Pa and the boys 'cause they'll be good and hungry after fixing up that old barn."

"Are we really gonna have a milk cow?"

"Comes with the property. That's what Mr. Boyd said. And some chickens too."

Sally sighed. "We have a lot of work to do."

"Yes, we do, honey, but that's okay 'cause we'll finally be building something that's gonna be ours."

"Will we be like the butterflies in the woods? Will we be able to stay here forever?"

"Yes, honey, it's different this time. We won't just be working this land for somebody else. We'll be slowly buying it. If we work hard, one day this will be the Novak farm." She squeezed Sally and laughed. "And that's why we're gonna plant us a flower garden. 'Cause we're gonna be here to see it bloom."

"But Pa says that fall's blowing in and then winter will be coming."

Jana shook her head. "Your Pa is wrong. The weather may get cold, but winter ain't coming for us ever again."

"It ain't?"

A breeze blew the intensifying nighttime scent of the honeysuckle to Jana, and she suddenly straightened her spine, held Sally at arms' length, and peered through the dusk at her upturned face. "Don't say *ain't*, Sally. Say *isn't*."

"But you said *ain't*."

"For the last time." Jana lifted her chin. "I won't say it again, and neither will you."

"Why not?"

"It isn't good English. Educated folk don't say it, and you're gonna be educated."

Sally's eyes sparkled so brightly they illuminated her face, and she broke free of her mother's hands and began jumping up and down. "You mean I can learn to read?"

Jana laughed and pulled Sally close again. "Yes! You're gonna learn to read and to write. You're gonna learn how to spell words and do sums. You're gonna learn everything I know. I want more for my girl, and I aim to have it!"

Chapter Ten

Christine Boyd ignored the boys' grumbling and tucked them into bed before dark. When she descended the stairs, Josie tried once again to get her to sit down and eat supper.

"I will wait for Mr. Boyd to come home," Christine answered as she picked up a fan from the hall table and headed for the front door. "I am going outside for a walk in the garden."

"You ain't got no hat on!"

"The sun is down. I will be fine."

"Don't you go pulling on no weeds or cutting no flowers without your gloves."

Christine shook her head with mock gravity. "I would not think of committing such a dastardly deed."

Josie's eyebrows shot up. "I think you better go sit in the parlor. You ain't making good sense to me."

Christine shook her head and pushed the screen door open. She smiled at the sight of the lightning bugs sending their tiny beacons of joy into the gathering dusk. The warm breeze wafting across the porch was soft against her delicate skin and carried the scent of roses and honeysuckle. She fingered the intricate design of a white, wicker rocker, plumped its embroidered pillows, and considered sitting. The breeze increased, sending the hanging ferns into a graceful dance, and Christine thought she sensed a cooling of the air. The last glow in the sky caught the frilled edges of the pink roses in the garden, and she couldn't resist their charm. She descended the steps, and encouraged by the increasing number of golden lights appearing in the dusky air, wandered across the velvet lawn until she reached the rose bed.

What an enchanting display. The delicate petals waved in the breeze, catching the gold and peach tones of the sunset. Christine turned and looked back at her home. The garden was layered with tall hollyhocks, roses, bellflowers, and lantana. It was magical in the fading light, but it was the house itself that stole the show. Christine admired the elegance of the home Richard had built for her, the welcome of the wrap-around porch. Lamps glowed in the parlor windows; she could see her piano waiting for her. *To think that I have been given all this when others have nothing.*

Impatience seeped into her; she desperately wanted Richard to return and tell her what had happened with Jana Novak's family. Christine's boys were safely asleep upstairs; she prayed that that remarkable little girl, Sally, was also safely asleep. She wanted—no, needed—to know that this one family had been saved. Her day had been filled with sights of human suffering. They had all impacted her painfully, but helping Jana was her best hope for having kept her promise to God. The promise she had made twenty years ago when she was about Sally Novak's age.

"Is it any cooler out here?" It was Richard coming down the front walk.

"You are home!" She clapped her hands together.

"I'm home." He took her in his arms. "Just where I want to be."

"Tell me everything!"

He laughed quietly and teased her. "I thought you were waiting for me, but all you want is news."

"Have you saved them?"

"I have done what I can do. They will have to save themselves, with God's help."

"But you got them away from that horrible landlord?"

"I did." He kissed her lips and stroked her cheek with his fingers. "Such beautiful skin."

She laughed and pulled back. "Don't tease me. Tell me exactly what happened."

"It will cost you another kiss...."

She threw her arms around his neck, kissed him soundly, then demanded, "Talk!"

"Well, the simple version is I took our overseer and two large wagons out to that shanty, and I convinced Kazimir Novak that I desperately needed his help because one of my tenants had up and left without notice. He agreed to go to work for me; we packed their pathetic belongings in the wagons and moved the whole family over to the old Hawkins farm I just bought."

"You lied?"

Richard shrugged his shoulders. "Men like Kazimir Novak have their pride too. I had to make him believe he was doing me a favor."

Christine smiled up at him. "You are the most wonderful man! Don't worry; God will understand. But what about the man Mr. Novak was working for? Will he be angry?"

"Probably, but when I run into him tomorrow, I'll just remind him that slave labor is illegal these days. He hasn't paid Novak a cent all summer, and that makes me wonder how he is treating his other tenants."

"How can you be sure you'll run into him?"

"I will make a point of it."

"Will he withdraw his account from the bank?"

"Not likely. We hold the mortgage on his land." He put his arm around her shoulders and turned her toward the house. "Let's forget all that for now. I want to tell you how proud I am of you."

"Why?"

"Because you have kept your promise to God."

"Yes, with your help I have. Oh, Richard!" Tears filled her eyes as she gazed at their house. "Look how much God has blessed us with. We have our home, our family, and all the security we could wish for."

"And tonight, thanks to your willingness to help, the Novak family has been given a fresh start."

Christine put her arm through his and snuggled closer. "You know what thrills me the most?"

"No. What?"

"That little girl, Sally. There's something quite remarkable about that child. Mark my word, Richard; we haven't seen the last of her in this town."

If you liked Christine's Promise,
you will love

Skirting Tradition,

the first full-length novel in the Aspiring Women Series.

Czech immigrant, Sarah Novak has an impossible dream. To become a school teacher of all things! Everyone in Riverford, Texas, will tell you that in 1895, immigrant farm girls do not become teachers. It's an absurd notion, and the sooner it's squashed, the better. These things can get out of hand, you know.

Girls like Sarah are supposed to marry young, birth strong sons, and slave from dawn-to-dark alongside their sharecropper husbands. That's the way it's always been, and that's why Sarah's father has already picked out her husband—a man Sarah detests. On the other hand, there's a handsome young banker, Robert Lee Logan. ... Well, that's a different story entirely.

Riverford has another problem—a troublesome newcomer named Victoria Hodges. She's a bohemian non-conformist, who ran off to Europe twenty-five years ago to become an artist. How she managed to hook wealthy local businessman, Hayden Hodges, is more than a body can understand. One thing's for certain. She's a corrupting force who must be removed from decent society.

Fortunately, Edith Bellows knows how to nip these things in the bud. A united stand of all the ladies, a cold-shouldered shut-out of such radicalism—that's the ticket.

But Mrs. Bellows barely gets her campaign underway when mutiny in the ranks occurs. Why on earth would genteel Christine Boyd, daughter of famed Confederate General Gibbes of Charleston, SC, befriend those two reprobates? Bless her heart! Doesn't she understand that the very lifeblood of southern womanhood—propriety—is at stake?

There will be no skirting of tradition on Mrs. Bellows' watch!

Or will there?

Skirting tradition

Chapter 1

Fall 1895

"It don't make no sense to educate a girl, Sally." Pa slammed his empty coffee cup on the farmhouse kitchen table. "No sense at all."

"But, Pa, if the boys get to go to school—"

"Boys need some book learning. They might make something of themselves. You ain't gonna do nothing but get married and have babies."

"I'm going to do a lot more! I'm not like Mama and the other girls. I want—"

"*Blaznivy!* Crazy talk. Marriage and children—that's why women were made, and you gotta accept that. You're gonna be seventeen soon, and you'll be ready to marry. And ain't no man gonna want a girl that's smarter than he is."

"But I don't want to marry, Pa! I want to be called by my Christian name, Sarah. I want to be Miss Sarah Novak, schoolteacher."

"It's settled, girl! You're gonna be just plain Sally. We gotta keep up the mortgage payments on this farm, and we need cash money to do that. So starting today, you're gonna work for Mrs. Bellows until you marry one of the Sykora boys. Now get breakfast on the table. It's almost dawn, and I gotta go rouse the boys."

Sarah shoved the biscuits into the oven, but the minute Pa disappeared, she raced to the front door and flung it open. Desperate for fresh air, she ran to the edge of the porch and searched the heavens for the comfort of an encouraging star. Nothing but dank air greeted her. The humidity of East Texas had settled on the farm, thickening the air and hiding the heavens.

She heard a rustle behind her, followed by her mother's voice. "Go get yourself dressed, honey. Won't do to be late your first morning."

"But Pa means for me to do all I usually do here before I leave, and you have the new baby to—"

Her mother's firm hug silenced her. "No. This is your time, Sally, your chance. I know your pa won't let you go to school, but you're gonna be in town, and that's something. The Lord can do a lot with just a little if you work with Him. You go out there into the world and do your best to make your dreams come true! Do it for me, honey. My life stops on this farm, but yours doesn't have to. You understand?"

"Yes, yes, Mama, I understand." Tears welled up in Sarah's eyes. "And I'll never forget that you... that you ..."

"My daughter"—Mama slammed her fist down on the porch railing—"my daughter is gonna have more!"

Unable to speak, Sarah nodded as tears splashed down her cheeks.

"Now go! Get dressed. You got to be at Mrs. Bellows' house good and early." Her mother pushed her gently toward the door. "I'll fix you some breakfast."

"Oh, don't bother about me, Mama. I'm too nervous to eat."

"Sally!" Pa called from the house. "Ain't nothing ready but the coffee. You're gonna have three hungry brothers down here any minute, looking for hot biscuits."

"Sally's got the biscuits in the oven," Mama announced as she preceded Sarah through the door.

Pa's chin jerked up at the sight of her. "Now, see here, Jana. You oughta be resting or nursing little Kazi. I don't want you taking on the chore of fixing breakfast."

"We don't always get what we want, do we?" Mama glared at him. "As for a newborn babe, I believe I can be the judge of what he needs. I've had plenty of experience." She jerked out the pan of biscuits, plopped two on a plate, and poured a cup of coffee. Handing both to Sarah, she said, "Take this upstairs with you, honey, and eat every crumb. And put your hair up. You're going to be working in town from now on, not on this farm, and you need to look like a town girl."

Pa's face darkened as Sarah took the food and hurried away.

When she returned ten minutes later, three sleepy boys were gathered around the table, complaining about going to school.

"Doesn't Sally look pretty with her hair up?" Mama asked as she kissed her daughter good-bye. "Just perfect for her first day working in town."

"*Dost je dost dela.* Pretty is as pretty does," Pa growled as he waved Sally out the door. "Let's get on with it; we both got work to do." He walked a ways with her in silence, then stopped and stared off at the horizon while Sarah waited.

"I'm countin' on you, Sally, to make us some cash money. We got that payment we owe the Boyds on the land coming due next week. And I ain't forgotten your mama's birthday is coming up." He pushed a knapsack into Sally's arms. "This here's some honey Mrs. Bellows wants to buy. See if you can get her to pay you for it today." He held out his hand with a few coins in it. "Take this money, add what you get for the honey, and buy your mama enough material to make a church dress."

"I'll do my best, Pa." Sarah looked at the woefully small amount. "Maybe I can find a sale."

"Just stretch it far as you can, girl." He stared sadly at the ground as he carved the dirt with the toe of his boot. "Now get on with you, and don't you be forgetting who you are. You're a farm girl. That's all."

In spite of the quick pace Sarah kept up and the morning's mugginess, she was invigorated by the three-mile walk into town. The mere thought of a day away from the farm was cause for joy. *Free!* After weeks confined to the scorching farm with its endlessly repetitive, mind-numbing tasks, her spirits soared. She gave in to her urge to twirl in a circle. Flinging her arms wide, she chanted, "Free, free! Free to be me!"

Sarah mounted the last rise, and the lazy, drifting river came into sight as it flowed through Riverford, Texas. A bustling place where cotton exchanges created wealth, town was Sarah's only experience of life outside the farm. All her dreams centered on it; there she could gain the experience necessary to lift her out of farm drudgery and rigid definitions of what her life must be. In short, Riverford, Texas, represented hope to Sarah Novak.

She hurried down the hill and progressed into town. Pausing in front of the school building, she longingly studied the open windows of the classrooms, trying to guess what subjects were taught in each room.

"Literature, history, certainly science and mathematics," she murmured. "And music. Maybe even art! If only I could—"

Her dream halted as Pa's last words blazed through her memory. *Don't you be forgetting who you are. You're a farm girl.* Sarah took one last look at the school. "Not for me," she whispered as she turned away, tears burning her eyes. "Cash money for the mortgage and Mama's dress—that's what I've got to focus on. Got to find Mrs. Bellows' house." Whipping herself into action, she marched down Main Street, resolved to put away her dreams and deal with the reality of her life.

Passing Hodges Department Store, she allowed herself a quick glimpse at the fashions displayed in the windows. "Too expensive," she cautioned herself as she hastily turned the corner toward Austin Avenue, "but I've got to find something special, something—"

Sarah's breath flew out of her, knocked out by something so dense it jarred her whole body. Gasping for air, knees buckling, she fell to the boardwalk. Seconds later, a male's anxious voice spoke words she couldn't quite comprehend. Someone clumsily brushed her hair off her face. "I'm so sorry!" The deep voice became intelligible to her. "Miss, are you hurt? Can you hear me?"

"Yes," she murmured as she struggled to focus on the face that floated above her. "Yes, I hear you." She attempted to sit up, but dizziness overcame her, and she sank back to the boardwalk.

"Wait! Let me help." A strong hand cradled her head while an arm wrapped around her shoulder blades. She felt herself being lifted into a sitting position. Hand trembling, she rubbed her forehead and willed her dizziness to pass.

"Do you feel faint?" The man crouched down beside her, cupping her face in his hands as he anxiously peered into her eyes. "Shall I send for the doctor?"

"No—no-o," Sarah stammered. Her vision cleared, and she realized she was staring at close range into soft brown eyes set in a concerned but distinctly handsome face.

"Is the girl all right?" someone nearby asked.

"Are you?" he leaned even closer, and a mysterious warmth rushed through Sarah and heated her cheeks.

"Yes!" She pulled back and struggled to stand.

The man sprang to his feet.

Strong hands lifted her, and to hide her strange feelings, she busied herself by straightening her dress.

"I'm so sorry," the young man said. "This is all my fault. I was reading the headlines—"

"Good job, Lee!" Another young man laughingly called out as he sauntered forward. "Your first morning back, and you flatten one of the local farm girls."

"This is no joking matter, brother!" the penitent man retorted. "Make yourself useful; pick up the newspaper while I help the lady to a bench."

"No!" Sarah protested. "I must go. Thank you very much, Mr. ...Mr. ..."

"Logan. Lee Logan. Miss..."

"Novak," Sarah offered as she suddenly remembered Mrs. Bellows. "I must go. I'll be late—oh, no! What's happened to the honey I was carrying?"

"Is this it?" The laughing man held up Sarah's knapsack.

"Yes. Oh, it's not broken, is it?"

"Don't feel anything sticky." He grinned at her. "Guess that's a good sign."

Lee Logan snatched the knapsack from his brother, inspected it carefully, and handed it to Sarah. "I think your honey is quite safe, Miss Novak, but I'm deeply concerned about you. I hope you will allow me to deliver you to your destination."

"We haven't got time for that kind of gallantry, big brother. I gotta get back to campus."

"Quiet, Walter!" Lee commanded, then softened his tone. "I assure you, Miss Novak, I am totally at your service, and I insist on seeing you safely home."

"All the way out to the country?" His brother laughed. "Granted, she is a knockout, but—"

"That's enough, Walter!" Lee cut his brother's comment off. "Please ignore my ill-mannered younger brother. The family is hopeful that a few years in college may mature him."

"Not if I can help it!" Walter stepped closer to Sarah and rudely examined her face. "Yep! A real knockout," he proclaimed. "Say, Lee's just here for the week, but I'm available any time. Just come on over to the men's dormitory—"

Sarah's confusion changed to fury. "I must go! Thank you, Mr. Lee Logan, for your kind offer, but I assure you I can take care of myself." She glared contemptuously at Walter Logan before adding. "And given my present company, I'd rather do just that."

Snatching the knapsack from Lee's hands, Sarah turned on her heel and did her best to march away with her head held high.

"Walter!" She heard Lee Logan's furious voice. "How could you say such a thing to a lady?"

"She's just a farm girl. Great figure, though, and that mass of hair ..."

Mortified, Sarah picked up her pace, and three blocks later she turned onto Austin Avenue, the most fashionable street in town. It was only then that she allowed herself to stop to catch her breath and dab at the angry tears dotting her face. Austin Avenue was a grand boulevard with a strip of manicured park running down the center, and here Sarah found a bench and sank down. She had a violent headache, but most of her suffering resulted from her confusion of feelings. Walter Logan's words had stung her to the core. *Just a farm girl.* On the other hand, she was at a loss to explain the excitement and comfort she had felt in Lee Logan's arms. Just the thought of him sent a delicious shiver down her spine.

In time, Sarah's good sense took over, and she tidied her hair and left behind the quiet of the park. Grand house after grand house presented themselves to Sarah's impressionable eyes as she struggled to imagine the lives of those who resided in such wealth. "It's another world," she breathed. "So ordered, so elegant and serene."

Several blocks later, Sarah saw the grandest house she had ever seen. Even though it was surrounded by a garden that covered most of that block of Austin Avenue, its tall, white pillars shone in the morning sun and beckoned her to enter the gate. She glanced up at the wrought-iron arch above the entrance. *Hodges House.* The letters were worked into the curve in an elegant script. Sarah sighed and continued down the block until she reached the more modest home next door. On the wooden gate, she found a simple sign with the word *Bellows* painted on it. She paused for a long moment, gulped down her sudden anxiety, then forced herself to enter the yard and walk toward the elaborate facade of the Victorian house. The closer she came, the more amazed she was by the seemingly endless gingerbread ornamentation. The house looked like a huge wedding cake covered in frosting curlicues.

Should I go around back? She stared up at the wide porch with its assortment of wicker furniture. The front door was open, with just a screen door keeping out the flies, and that bit of casualness gave her courage. She climbed the steps and knocked.

"What you want here?" a Negro woman demanded when she came to the door.

"May I please speak to Mrs. Bellows?"

The woman scornfully looked Sarah up and down. "What business you got with Miz Edith? What you got in that knapsack?"

"It's honey for Mrs. Bellows."

"Well, I'll just take that." The woman pushed open the screen door. "Ain't no need for the likes of you to be bothering Miz Edith."

Sarah stepped back and held the honey behind her. "I need to collect the money for it, and I'm supposed to begin working for Mrs. Bellows today."

"Miz Edith pay you when she get 'round to it." The large woman held out her hand for the pot of honey. "And she don't need no more help."

"But I'm supposed to—"

"What in the name of heaven is going on, Ada?" a woman demanded from inside the house. "You know very well that you are supposed to be cleaning the library before Mr. Bellows comes home from Fort Worth. He simply cannot abide having his things in disorder. I've already told you I want every one of those books dusted."

"Well, this girl done come to the door with some honey, Miz Edith, and stop me in my tracks."

Mrs. Bellows came into sight as she declared, "Seems to me you're mighty easy to stop in your tracks, Ada, when there's fall cleaning to be done. Now get back to work!"

"Yes'm," Ada muttered as she turned and disappeared down the main hall.

Sighing dramatically, Mrs. Bellows dragged herself out onto the porch. "Is it any wonder I have the migraine with help like that?"

Uncertain what to say, Sarah stood silently, her own head aching, while Mrs. Bellows flung her ample body down on a settee. "Lord knows, I'm not the kind to complain, but Ada's just short of a curse. A body tries to be a Christian, of course, and help her kind out, but surely a body has a right to expect a little work in exchange. Now, what is it you want?"

"I'm here to work for you, Mrs. Bellows, like you and Pa arranged. And I brought the honey you wanted to buy."

"Oh, you're Kazimir's girl! Such an odd name...Kazimir."

"It's Czech, ma'am."

"Well, *I* know that, but it just seems to me that if he wants to be an American—"

"He is an American, ma'am, but he was born—"

Mrs. Bellows waved her hand. "Best forget all that foreign stuff. Why, I always say—oh, never you mind. I've seen you at church. Sally, isn't it?"

"I prefer to be called Sarah, ma'am, if you don't mind."

"You've really grown up in the last year, Sally. I expect you'll be marrying soon, heaven help you! How's your mama doing?"

Sarah opened her mouth to respond, but before she could utter a word, Edith Bellows babbled on, "Bless her heart! Another baby, I hear. And after losing all those others. How many was it? You'd think a body would quit tempting fate after a while, but I reckon you country folk just breed like rabbits."

Sarah clamped her teeth together.

"Well, just leave the honey right there on that table, and I'll have that worthless Ada put it in the kitchen. She ought to be able to accomplish that!"

"If I could collect the money for it, ma'am, before I leave this afternoon, I'd sure appreciate it. You see, my mother's birthday is coming up, and my pa wants to buy her a present."

"What in heaven's name does he want to buy that he needs so much money?"

"Some material, ma'am." Sarah struggled to hold back her anger. "And some trim."

"Trim?" Mrs. Bellows snorted. "Well, I suppose your poor mama deserves something for all she's been through."

"Yes, ma'am, so if I could just have the money before I leave..."

"Well, of course you can, Sally! Far be it from me to owe anyone a single penny and certainly not someone as needy as your family. Why, everyone in this town knows I'm the first one, the very first one, to help the needy. But oh! This migraine is killing me!"

Sarah flushed hot with anger.

"Well, never mind. No one knows how much I suffer, and I'm certainly not going to tell anyone." Mrs. Bellows rose slowly from the settee and tugged at the bodice that strained to cover her ample bosom. "I declare! You'd think a dressmaker who gets paid what I pay Mrs. Bettis could fit a bodice properly! It's not as if she didn't have plenty of fabric. I never skimp on dress goods, and I'll certainly never adopt the flimsy styles of you know who."

Confused, Sarah stared at Mrs. Bellows until the loquacious woman jerked her head to the left and whispered, "Her, of course!"

When Sarah turned to look, Mrs. Bellows hissed, "Don't look, Sally! Lord a mercy! Don't you know anything? She'll know we're watching her, and I for one don't intend to give her the slightest notice. I don't care if she did marry Hayden Hodges!"

"Oh." Sarah began to put the pieces together. "I heard he married a woman named Victoria from Galveston."

"From Galveston?" Mrs. Bellows snorted. "I only wish that's where he found her. She has spent the last twenty-five years in Europe!"

"Really? How exciting!"

"Exciting? Hardly! And to think he replaced sweet Melinda—God rest her soul—with an artist from Europe! The point is, the ladies of Riverford have got to stand united against the intrusion of the vulgarities of foreign places. Though how we're going to do it when it moves in right next door, I don't know! Well, don't just stand there, Sally! Come with me. You've got work to do."

Sarah watched as Mrs. Bellows tossed her bustle behind her and stormed through the screen door. When she followed, Sarah found herself in a large, high-ceilinged room with an ornately carved oak staircase ascending the left side. "Stay here," Mrs. Bellows ordered. "I must take something for my splitting head, and I won't have you wandering through the house."

"I wouldn't—"

As Mrs. Bellows hurried down the hall talking to herself, a desperate groan from Sarah's left caught her attention, and she walked over and peered into the room. Ada was reaching up as high as she could, swiping a dust cloth at a shelf above her head. "This gonna be the death of me," she grumbled as she slapped the cloth across the spine of the books.

"Stop that!" Sarah's passionate love of books forced the words to her tongue. "That's no way to treat books, and you'll certainly never get them clean that way."

"*Hmmp!*" Ada snorted. "What you know about books anyway? Bet you can't even read."

"I certainly can!" Sarah retorted as she raced into the room. "Here. You can use this ladder to get to the high shelves." She pulled the rolling ladder toward Ada.

"I knows that, but I ain't climbing no ladder." Ada turned back to the shelves and began whipping the books again.

"Then I'll do it!" Sarah scampered up the ladder and turned to Ada. "Hand me up a rag."

"Miz Edith ain't gonna like you comin' in here, girl."

"Mrs. Edith likes it very much!" Mrs. Bellows' voice boomed so loudly from the door that Sarah almost fell off the ladder. "Ada, I declare! You're the most worthless help I've ever had the misfortune to hire. You're good for nothing except kitchen work. Why, this poor little country girl knows more than you do about cleaning!"

"Yes'm." Ada hung her head but cut her eyes angrily toward Sarah.

"Well, get on back to the kitchen where you belong then!"

"Yes'm."

"And as for you, Sally, I want you to begin work by dusting every one of those books and cleaning the shelves under them. This room has to be perfect before Mr. Bellows comes home from Fort Worth. I am *not* able to endure another one of his hissy fits!"

Her headache completely forgotten, Sarah scampered down the ladder and grabbed the dust rags. "You'll see; it'll be all spanking clean, Mrs. Bellows. I love books, and I—"

"No chatter, Sally! Just work." Mrs. Bellows pressed her finger to her forehead. "This migraine is going to be the death of me."

"You better go lie down, Mrs. Bellows," Sarah soothed as she briskly pulled books from the shelves and dusted them. "Maybe out on the porch where it's cooler, and maybe Ada should bring you some lemonade."

"What a thoughtful girl you are, Sally!"

"You want me to call Ada for you?"

"No, I'll call her myself, the lazy girl." Mrs. Bellows tossed her bustle to the back as she turned away. "Ada! Where are you? I declare you are never in the right place at the right time! A-a-da-a?"

Sarah hugged herself for joy. "All these books!" she breathed. "Just look at them!"

She worked diligently for over an hour before movement in the garden next door caught her eye. Scurrying down the ladder, she glanced over her shoulder to be certain Mrs. Bellows wasn't in the hall and then hurried to the window. A little gasp of wonder escaped her lips at the sight of a tall, red-haired lady dressed in a strange costume. "Why, her skirt's all curled under," Sarah whispered, "and—oh goodness—it's divided into two parts!" With wide, graceful movements of her arms, the lady directed several men around the yard as if she were directing a choir. "That's gotta be the new Mrs. Hodges. Victoria from Galveston. She's so beautiful, so confident!" A smile germinated deep inside Sarah and blossomed on her face. "I like her!"

"Sally! Come away from that window at once!" Mrs. Bellows ordered from the hall. "It's perfectly natural at your age that you would be fascinated by such lurid behavior," she continued as she waddled into the room, "but you must resist the temptation."

As Sarah raced back to the bookshelves, Mrs. Bellows hastened to the window to watch her neighbor.

"Can you believe it? Not the slightest bow to modesty in that woman's dress. No drape whatsoever, not even a flounce to cover her...her...backside. Scandalous!" She leaned so close to the window that her nose banged into the glass, forcing Sarah to choke down a giggle but not stopping Mrs. Bellows' tongue. "Out there ordering men around like a...like a general or something! Who does she think she is? What an example to set for impressionable young minds like yours! I must defend you from this onslaught against femininity!" Mrs. Bellows jerked the shade down.

Sarah grinned at the leather-covered spines in front of her. "Yes, ma'am," she choked out.

"It's essential that even a farm girl like you have proper models." Mrs. Bellows snatched the side of the shade back and continued her spying. "Your mama, poor thing, can hardly be expected to guide you, but I can. Yes, indeed, I can!" Clucking her tongue, she shook her head in disgust. "What is the world coming to? Riverford is doomed. Doomed, I tell you! Drastic measures must be taken to defend the younger generation."

"Sally!" Mrs. Bellows whirled around from the window so quickly she made Sarah jump. "You have my permission, as of this moment, to consider me your role model, though it will, of course, be a great burden to me."

"Thank you, ma'am." Sarah tried to smile gratefully.

"It's no more—and no less—than my duty." Mrs. Bellows stood taller and jerked her bodice down. "Anyone in town will tell you that

I never shirk my duty." She pulled a handkerchief from her bosom and began running the white linen over the surfaces Sarah had dusted. "A good job," she finally concluded. "Under my tutelage, you could become an acceptable maid." She paused and screwed up her face in thought. "Yes! My duty is apparent to me. I must teach you how to be the best maid Riverford has ever seen. It will be your life's work, your destiny, and I will have made it possible."

Sarah's mouth fell open.

"Close your mouth, girl!" Mrs. Bellows ordered. "Or you'll catch flies."

"Ma'am, my pa plans for me—"

"I've no doubt that your pa will see the good sense of your committing your life to such noble service, and it's no secret that he could use the money, although it certainly won't be full wages while you're in training. You do understand that, don't you? Well, of course you do," she rattled on. "Why, I'll go right this minute and write a note to your father explaining my plan. I know my duty, and anyone in town will tell you…" Her voice trailed off as she jerked her bustle around and waddled out of the library.

Sarah stood perfectly still for a moment, stunned by the radical change in her life that Mrs. Bellows was suggesting, indeed ordering. "But I don't want to be a maid," she whispered, cringing at the very thought. She turned to the window and remembered Mrs. Hodges' graceful but commanding presence, and her perspective began to change. "It would mean being in town, though… and money… and all these books. Maybe I could even…" She shook her head violently to clear her mind of her personal dreams and returned to the bookshelves with a vengeance.

When Sarah finally finished her long day of housework, she pocketed the money Mrs. Bellows had paid her for the honey and exited out the back door as ordered. She retraced her early morning steps through the town and began the steady climb up the hill away from the river. The setting sun cast fascinating shadows across the dirt road and mellowed the dry fields as she hurried home.

Sarah's physical tiredness was overwhelmed by her excitement as she finally allowed herself to imagine spending her days in town. *Mrs. Bellows will be a trial, but to be surrounded by the fine things in her house... all that china and crystal and grand old furniture—but most of all the books. Oh, the books!* Images of leather-bound volumes floated through her mind, but quite unexpectedly the memory of warm brown eyes and strong hands sent thoughts of books flying. *Lee Logan... hmmm...*

Order your copy of "Skirting Tradition" today!

Acknowledgements

Thank you, Diana Flegal, for believing in my God-given writing talent and especially for suggesting that I write this novella. You are more than my literary agent; you are my friend and sister in Christ.

Many thanks to Elizabeth Kim, of Hartline Literary Agency, for her encouragement, creativity, and attention to detail in the production of this book. I am especially thankful for Elizabeth's patience and loving support when a death in my family delayed my work.

Thank you KATies, my Advance Team of 54 ladies, for your support and enthusiasm about every detail of this book. You are a joy!

Thank you Hearties! Your support of faith-friendly, family-friendly entertainment is changing the world. I am blessed to have you as fans and friends. You give me hope for the future and keep me writing.

Last, but definitely not least—Chan Strong, Jan Childs, and Lou Beasley. Thank you for loving me, accepting me just as I am, supporting my crazy writing career, and dragging me away from the computer on occasion. You are the best friends I could ever wish for.

About the Author

Kay Moser is a native of historic Nacogdoches, Texas, a small town deep in the piney woods of East Texas. She earned a Ph.D. degree from Baylor University, specializing in 19th century literature. She was a professor of literature for many years and is currently a full-time novelist. Her sixth novel, "Skirting Tradition," releases in January, 2017.

If you enjoyed *Christine's Promise*, you may also enjoy other novels by Kay Moser:

The Celebration Series

Celebration!
Rachel D'Evereau has everything the world can offer—wealth and prestige, striking beauty, a successful husband, and a profession she loves. Yet, when a series of catastrophes begin to shatter the secure, comfortable walls that surround her life, she is forced to admit long-suppressed feelings of insecurity and worthlessness.

Rachel returns to her ancestral plantation home where she confronts the painful secrets that have haunted and challenged members of her family for generations. Her quest to rekindle the spiritual flames that guided her as a child take her on an unexpected journey, a journey from darkness into light.

Celebration! is a sweeping saga filled with characters whose lives blaze across the pages of history, from the genteel South of the early 1800's to the tumultuous landscapes of modern America. It is also a powerful and moving novel that captures the journey each of us must take if we are to accept our true identity as God's worthy children.

Glimpse of Splendor
Forever changed by a bullet, international journalist Mark Goodman redefines success: Live life—Walk again—Return home to Louisiana to claim his first and only love, Rachel D'Evereau.

Recently widowed, Rachel has returned to her ancestral plantation, Belle St. Marie, to search for peace.

Finally healed of his injury, Mark plans a surprise visit home to claim his beloved. The time is perfect. Or so Mark thinks.

Upon his arrival, he encounters obstacles he never expected. A political race endangers his family's longstanding honor. Rachel's dysfunctional family and the infidelity of her deceased husband have left her feeling worthless, detached from God, and ready to marry Louis Simone, a wealthy suitor who offers her a life of ease.

Has Mark arrived in time?

Will Rachel find the true basis of her worth and be freed to love again?

Set against the backdrop of Louisiana's intriguing 20th century plantation culture, *Glimpse of Splendor* engulfs the reader in the sustained wind of steadfast love—both human and divine, the cleansing breeze of forgiveness, and the roar of Louisiana politics.

The Charleston Series

Counterfeit Legacy

Caroline Bradford Randolph is a Dallas socialite who has discovered that neither her wealth nor the legacy of her famous Charleston, S.C. ancestors can satisfy her deepest longings. When a freakish storm gives Caroline the chance to hold the most cherished Bradford heirloom in her hands for the first time, she discovers that it contains a secret that may well destroy the prestigious legacy of the Bradfords. Since Caroline has based her life on this legacy, hard choices loom ahead for her.

Should she cover up her discovery in order to protect her marriage to wealthy industrialist David Randolph? Or should she investigate the truth of her proud ancestry in hopes of finding the fulfillment she so desperately needs?

Counterfeit Legacy will captivate you as you travel with Caroline through the trials and questions of her contemporary life into the secrets of her ancestors.

David's Gift

David Randolph, owner of an international corporation, is one of Dallas' most admired men. His enormous wealth and power give him control over thousands of lives, including that of his beautiful wife,

Caroline. From Texas to London to Tokyo, David wields his power ruthlessly just as his father taught him to.

However, behind his facade of bravado, David is crumbling and tormented by nightmares.

What is disturbing him so drastically? Why the anxiety, the doubts, the shattered self-image?

Only David knows the truth about his first marriage and the death of his first wife, Danielle.

Can he continue to hide the truth about his past deeds from Caroline? If he does, will be miss out on the greatest gift of his life?

Can anyone or anything teach David that happiness grows from one's center to one's surface and that joy comes only when one gives oneself away?

Stay tuned for the
Aspiring Women Series

Skirting Tradition
Ruffling Society

Try these other titles by Hartline authors:

Molly Noble Bull's *The Rogue's Daughter*
Had she really stood in front of God and church and minister, and allowed herself to be joined to Seth Matthews for life?

In 1890 and a short time after graduating from a college for teachers in San Antonio, Texas, Rebecca Roberts found herself with both the teaching job she desperately needed and something else she had been determined never to have—a husband. Seth Matthews, a rugged, independent widower, had hired Rebecca to teach his three children, then married her "to save her reputation." It was a legal arrangement only, no love involved.

Or was there?

The azure skies, sun-baked earth, and majestic live oaks of Seth's south Texas ranch afford the setting for the most important lessons of this story. Rebecca learns about trust and tenderness, and Seth learns about the God she loves.

Lena Nelson Dooley's *The Gold Digger*
It's 1890, and Golden, New Mexico, is a booming mining town where men far outnumber women. So when an old wealthy miner named Philip Smith finds himself in need of a nursemaid, he places an ad for a mail-order bride—despite the protests of his friend Jeremiah. Hoping to escape a perilous situation back East, young Madeleine Mercer answers the ad and arrives in town under a cloud of suspicion. But just as she begins to win over Philip—and Jeremiah himself—the secrets she left behind threaten to follow her to Golden...and tarnish her character beyond redemption.

Lena Nelson Dooley's *The Gold Digger*

Because of an earlier betrayal, Franklin vows never to open his heart to another woman. But he desires an heir.

When Lorinda is finally out from under the control of men who made all the decisions in her life, she promises herself she will never allow a man to control her again. But how can she provide for her infant son?

Marriage seems like the perfect arrangement until two people from Franklin's past endanger Lorinda. How can he save her? And how will this affect the way they feel about each other?